MALE VIRGIN

MALE VIRGIN

JOHN B. THOMPSON & JACK WOODFORD

CUTTING EDGE

ISBN-13: 978-1-954840-60-7

Published by
Cutting Edge Books
PO Box 8212
Calabasas, CA 91372
www.cuttingedgebooks.com

CHAPTER ONE

APPLIED PSYCHOLOGY

NEVER knew how we both got on the floor, but there we were. And all because of a kiss.

I know I didn't trip. I think I must have blacked out momentarily when she sank a thumb into the muscle of my jaw, an excellent move to make the jaw relax. My jaw did, and I'm quite certain I fainted. Not really, of course, because I didn't completely lose consciousness, but I must have come very near it.

You must understand about that kiss. It was no ordinary kiss. I must hasten to add that it was Miss Cannon who did the kissing, and never in my most flamboyant dreams would I have pictured such a vision of loveliness in my arms.

I remember well how it all began ...

I was holding my afternoon classes in Psychology Two in the science building. The students were considerably more attentive than usual due to the subject matter. This had to do with certain psychological anomalies which often have bizarre sexual manifestations, a portion of the lesson which I would have been delighted to delete entirely as I am a bachelor and have a distinct aversion to speaking about such things with the frankness now forced upon one in a classroom by our young moderns. They are, to be brief, totally devoid in some cases of a sense of delicacy and are prone to bring up frightfully embarrassing problems which they expect me to solve or at least give an intelligent discourse about. Neither of these two alternatives attract me. Why a psychologist who is teaching for a living should be made the judge of all manner of digressions from accepted moral standards I cannot imagine. On some particularly mortifying occasions I have seen contempt in the eyes of my questioners and should it ever get around in the right places that Thomas McBride Tallant grew red in the face and blurted out what my students would call the brush-off, my fitness as an instructor might be questioned. On this particular day I had been—badgered, is the word that comes to me—by a Miss Cannon who had an interest in her subject which was, to say the least, excessive.

"Professor, would you say that this type of condition in a woman would be called nymphomania?"

I glanced at her quickly, then away, for reasons which will become apparent. "I would not like to venture an opinion on the subject, Miss Cannon. One gets far afield and such discussions are always filled with speculation. Let us, therefore, keep to the subject at hand." I turned my attention back to the class. "Now it has been successfully demonstrated that the perpetrator of what we read of as the sex crime is more often than not a constitutional psychopathic inferior. But you must understand that this condition has many manifestations…"

"Hollingshead agrees with me, Professor," said Miss Cannon.

"Then," I said, with what I hoped was a crushing squelch, "you and Hollingshead make a fine team."

Instead of being crushed, she smiled, and her eyes as usual amounted to an affront. The class ended soon afterward and with a sigh I sat down to make out my daily report, not even watching the students as they dawdled or rushed depending on whether they now had a vacant period or another class. Miss Cannon was one of the former and after the noise had subsided I was conscious that someone still remained but I was afraid to look. My intuition, forgive the term, was not amiss. It was she.

She rose to her feet with a movement that I can only describe as sinuous and approached the desk, her hips undulating in a manner that to some would have been provocative. She was not a small girl, and her legs I must admit were of surpassingly excellent construction, with the accent on sturdiness, as was the rest of her. She wore a light sweater and how it resisted the assault of her breasts I do not know. Her waist was small and her hips smoothly contoured, making in all, and from a purely esthetic point of view, a rather delightful picture.

"I would like to know why a psychologist is knocked for a row of onions everytime a question is asked off the beaten path? It has been my impression that psychologists are the proper ones to ask, yet the times I've asked, you have blushed and brushed. You always took a mental powder so to speak."

"Miss Cannon," I said, experiencing a strange weak feeling that both irritated and appalled me, "I have a job to do. I do it the way that to me seems best. I might point out that all your questions come very close to the indelicate and are not at all fitting in a class of mixed students."

A smile crept across her face revealing twin rows of strong and well-formed white teeth. I noticed at the same time that her lips were smooth and full, giving the impression of sensuality as did the rest of her.

"They said you were one of those," she said regretfully, "but I was hoping it wasn't so. Frankness embarrasses you, questions throw you ... ye gods, why did you ever take up psychology?"

"A most absorbing science," I retorted with heat.

"Not absorbing enough to take you from between the covers of a textbook. You know what I think, Prof?"

I admitted I did not.

"I think the reason my questions throw you is because you don't know the answers, except as put out by Hollingshead, Adler, Thorndike, James, et al. I don't believe that the life you are supposed to be teaching people to conquer has ever touched you. I believe that you have been sheltered, pampered, and intellectually emasculated. I believe you need a bit of life. Furthermore, I can prove it."

From the feeling of my face I knew I was blushing hotly which infuriated me as did her character analysis. "Miss Cannon, allow me to say that you are merely making noises through your mouth. You are talking sheerest speculation and you cannot prove a single thing you say."

"I think," she continued, looking me up and down as though considering buying me by the pound, "that you are an intellectual vacuum. A parrot repeating a long list of memorized theorems and findings, not one of which you could put to practical use, not one of which you can handle other than to fire it at us from behind a book."

In spite of my rage and resentment, I found, to my horror, that I had fixed my eyes on the neck of her sweater and the beginning of a little valley which, I knew from pictures, would grow deeper as it progressed downward. My horror was further heightened when I realized that the sight had caused some bizarre bodily reactions. With a deathlike grip on my faculties I faced her again. "You spoke," I said with a trembling sneer, "of proof. So far you have only been indulging in diatribe. Where, I pray, is this proof of yours?"

She smiled. Again I felt something like a shock to a sensitive nerve. "The proof will be forthcoming. I only wanted to make sure I had you sore enough to follow it through. Do you have a car?"

"I do not," I said severely. "I have no time for such things. Another question, Miss Cannon, if you dislike me so heartily, why do you not change to another instructor? It could be arranged you know."

"Who the hell said I didn't like you?"

I was frankly nonplussed.

"My scientific curiosity has nothing to do with personal like and dislike. I merely gave out with what I thought about you ducking questions, but a few changes here and there and you'd be an all right guy. You're tall, and if you weren't so stiff about the face you'd be fairly good-looking. Beneath that handsome tweed I suspect there runs plenty of muscle."

"I was once called the fastest human that ever ran the mile at Cornell," I assured her with some little pride. "I have boxed, and during the war I was considered adept at Judo."

"Bravo!" she applauded. "I can see where my proof might even prove diverting."

"If not a total failure," I supplied nastily. "When and where is this proof to take place?"

"Now!" she said, "I have a car and a good place in mind."

"Probably the only thing good you've ever had in your mind," I said malignantly, feeling that I had recovered some of my lost face.

She eyed me closely for a moment. "If I had a good psychiatrist here I could prove it right now," she said, "but my way will be more fun."

I had occasion to recall that remark before many hours had elapsed.

"My car is about a block down Dalton," she said. "Shall we go?"

"By all means," I said, fitting my hat carefully to my head. This is my last recollection of the hat. It was never found.

"I could use a sandwich," she announced. "Suppose we waltz around to a drive-in and have one before we vanquish you, but utterly?"

"Take any liberties with my time that please you," I retorted. "I have nothing to do but earn a living."

She drove out on St. Charles Street and whipped the coupe into an establishment where one could sit in one's vehicle and order, which Miss Cannon did. She ordered something she called a cheeseburger, the very name of which revolted me, and a drink which she commanded to be brought at once, the last name of which was Collins. I seem to remember that it had a first name; but it escapes me. Not wishing to appear a bump, I told the boy that I also desired a Collins, a decision which reaped a glance from Miss Cannon, which I could not at the moment interpret. The drinks came, and I must admit that except for a certain pungency which was not necessarily unpleasant the drink was most refreshing. It is made with lemon juice, sugar, and water, with a cherry at the bottom providing a festive air. A most attractive drink, and as I say, very stimulating. Miss Cannon finished her drink and started eating her cheeseburger which she seemed to relish. I, having refused to eat, ordered another Collins. It seemed even nicer than the first and by the time she had finished her milk and sandwich I had finished my third Collins and was aware of a sense of extreme well being.

"I feel impelled to remark, Miss Cannon," I said as we rolled away from the drive-in, "that you are in for a disappointment. Inasmuch as I bear you no malice you may drop me at State Street and I'll go home. I will allow you to forget the experiment." I was beginning to feel hungry by this time.

"Not on your life, Prof," she said exuberantly.

Her hair was the texture of silk and the skin of her face was even more so. I was astonished at myself. Twice in the course of one afternoon I had caught myself absorbed in her physical qualities, something I ordinarily do not observe because I think that such absorption is demoralizing, demeaning, and productive of fleshly thoughts. It is my opinion, further, that the essence of thought is not possible, that higher planes are unreachable, if one does not, to a great extent, set oneself apart from these things. Probably one reason for my reaching the age of thirty without having married is my pursuit of learning and my total abstinence from any contact with the female. I feel that in this my two maiden aunts who reared me did me a signal service and made it possible for me to achieve scholastic heights, not to mention heights of pure thought, which would not otherwise have been attainable.

Miss Cannon drove, as she walked, with a certain indefinable grace and coordinated control which made her body behave in a disturbing manner and her car behave perfectly.

"Why," I asked, "are you so determined to prove me a dim switch?" I had heard the term and it seemed apt at the time.

"The phrase is dim bulb," she said. "I am one of a rising species of woman who decry any waste in manhood. As I have pointed out, once the shell is cracked and the chick breathes good fresh air it might develop into a respectable rooster."

"Are you, by any chance, referring to me as a rooster?"

"By no means," she assured me. "As far as can be determined you are a capon with all the attendant deficiencies. It is only an experiment to determine if you are what I think you are or, Allah forbid, what you think you are. It is my considered opinion that you are not what you think you are, and had you the guts of a fly you'd behave otherwise."

"Has it not occurred to you," I said with commendable mildness, "that my background might offer a contradiction to what you believe me to be? I was, you know, reared in a God-fearing household by two maiden aunts who showed me higher things than those reached by the senses."

"Holy cow!" she said inelegantly. "Now I'm beginning to understand, and since I'm a better psychologist than you'll ever be, I'll give you my report Monday morning as to whether you'll ever amount to anything but a desiccated repository for dusty, mummified polemics."

"I do not consider myself such," I said stiffly. "I think I am a normal, if somewhat sensitive, human with my eye on a star rather than a dunghill...." I stopped, appalled at my coarse speech, but Miss Cannon laughed delightedly.

"Say, that was quite a remark. I'll have to remember it but what I want to know is whether you are really a constitutional star-gazer or a tumble bug with delusions of grandeur."

Miss Cannon's deft use of phraseology left a laugh trembling inside me which I subdued. I looked her over again, all the way from her trim ankles past her strong, but symmetrical calves, to her long, sturdy thighs. The smallness and trim lines of her waist held me for a moment, then the pouting pointed bulges of her breasts, which might be characterized as lush, took my eyes for more than their share of time. I was shocked when I found her watching me with a … yes, a grin.

"Like what you see, Prof?"

"I was in deep thought," I said, and it sounded prim even to me. "I have a habit of fixing my eyes on a given object when I feel the need for concentration."

"The time," she shot back, "is nearing. I live here and shall conduct my experiment in the privacy of my own little apartment."

"This whole thing has a most unsavory atmosphere," I said, feeling a stab of fright without knowing the exact cause of it.

"If you are too much of a sissy, go on back to your two maiden aunts and cry on their starved bosoms."

She seemed a little irked.

"I think this an excellent time to show you up for what you are," I said. "Let's get along with your experiment so that I may point out just where you fail."

"If I fail," she retorted, as she drove the car into a narrow driveway, "I won't need anyone to tell me why or wherefore."

The apartment was small but modern, colorful, and impeccably kept. Miss Cannon seated me on a powder-blue divan which was most comfortable.

"If you would make me a Collins I should be grateful. I seem to be dryer than when I had the last one." She gave me that queer glance again and disappeared into her kitchen. In a few minutes she reappeared with two Collins, replicas of the ones we had been served except that they were bigger and the stinging pungency was more pronounced.

"It must be the oil from the lemon peel."

"What?"

"This drink, I notice, has a certain pungency for which I cannot account and I suggested the possibility of it being the peel of lemon, the oil of which might produce this taste."

"That's exactly what it is, Prof, and don't let anyone tell you different."

Miss Cannon went into her bedroom—to change her clothes, I assumed, as the day had been warm and women love to change clothes upon any pretext, this being a Narcissistic drive which they all seem to share. When she came back I was shocked. I use that word because I can think of nothing stronger. She had brushed her soft blonde hair till it foamed about her shoulders in a cloud. She wore a house dress, I think it is called, long and fitting like no house dress has any business fitting. The Collins I had just drunk seemed to have distorted my vision somewhat and I found myself shaking my head to get a better view, although I was assailed with the conviction that I should take to my heels as a matter of precaution and let the experiment go to pot. But that would never do, I realized, as I'd never be able to face Miss Cannon in class again.

"I can tell you're concentrating again," she said, as she walked with her supple stride over to the couch and sat beside me. "And I know what you're concentrating on."

I regained my breath with difficulty and swallowed—noisily I'm afraid. "Miss Cannon, if it will give you any satisfaction, I'll admit that you have a perfect genius for making inappropriate remarks. I fear you are quite callous. You seem to take a keen delight in causing me discomfort."

"Now, Prof, be honest. Do I or do I not attract you?"

I struggled over this one for a moment, seeming a little slow-minded in spite of the soaring confidence which the last Collins had more than restored. "Again, if it affords you pleasure, I may say that I find you attractive, in the way that I would a flower, a tree, or a particularly succulent fruit."

"Now that last interests me. What would you do with an attractively succulent fruit if you had one right now and felt hungry?"

I was, in a manner of speaking, driven into a linguistic cul-de-sac. The only sensible answer was the very one I did not want to make. Still I felt that, so far, her experiment had not placed me in any particularly bad light, so I said, "I would eat it, of course. After properly washing and doing whatever else might be necessary... paring, peeling, and..." I stopped, because I saw that I had gone from a cul-de-sac into a pitfall.

She laughed a silvery laugh that made her throat do oddly attractive little things and made me forget, momentarily, the spot I was in. "I bathed when I changed," she said. "Shall I peel—or pare?"

"I was merely using a figure of speech," I said icily, "which anyone with the intelligence of a third-grade fruit—er, moron—would understand."

"What is Freud's opinion of the *lapsus linguae*?"

"It is fairly widely accepted that the slip of the tongue is the subconscious speaking forth...."

"Exactly. You slipped and said fruit, which proves that you are still considering me as a fruit. Now, I'd make an excellent banana and I could peel with the most stupefying grace...."

"Miss Cannon, I am a busy man. I have papers to grade. Pray get along with your so-called experiment so that I may go home. Let's dispense with facetiousness and try to be intelligent for a while."

She crept closer to me till I could actually feel the warmth of her body, her perfume floating about me in a cloud of the most frightening sweetness. Her eyes were on mine, serious, intent, and almost hypnotic. "Do you really want to be intelligent right now?"

"No!" I ejaculated with some force. "That is, yes—of course I do."

"The *lapsus linguae* again."

I winced because there was a modicum of truth in her words. She came closer and the quality of her skin made my mouth go dry and pucker. Her lashes were, I'm certain, more than half an inch long and her brown eyes seemed enormous. I could retreat no further without getting up and my pride made me discard this stratagem. Before I knew it she was closer than was comfortable; indeed, her proximity was decidedly uncomfortable.

"I really think I should go, Miss Cannon," I said weakly, attempting to rise.

"No!" I had heard words of command while in the service but nothing like that one word ever struck my ears. It deprived me of speech and locomotion and the look on her face started a war within me. From somewhere came an ardent desire to put my arms around her and clutch her close to me, to twine her hair in my hands and to say silly things to her. At this precise moment, showing that her boast of her knowledge of psychology was not entirely wrong, she slipped her arm around my neck and pulled me toward her. My brain protested wildly but this strange power rose higher and higher within me like a single clear note on a flute, crushing all resistance. Before I had time to make a concerted effort to regain my aplomb, her soft smooth lips touched mine, and something snapped within me. In no other way can I explain my actions. My arms went around her and with such strength that I'm afraid I hurt her, because she gave a little gasp.

It was then that I discovered that we were on the floor and I had both arms around her. I could hear myself saying:

"Womanlike, you had to disrupt my entire poise. I was quite..." I suddenly realized what a horrible position I was in. The girl was relaxed in my arms but her robe had come open at the waist and her long white legs were exposed almost to the hip. Again a gust of drunken power surged through me and I kissed her hard. My hands buried themselves in her hair, clutching its softness with a queer kind of savage eagerness. She caught one of my hands and pulling it away from her hair placed it between us, grasped the top of her robe and tugged it open. My hand touched her breast then and the thrumming of heated blood in my head almost made me swoon. Driven by a force which I had some time ago admitted as my superior, and in a clumsy effort to ease a somewhat uncomfortable position, my hand chanced to touch her thigh, sending a noticeable rigor through her. It was cool and satin smooth, reacting on the hot skin of my hand as would a cooling balm, something of an antithesis to other reactions throughout my body which were anything but soothing.

At this point I must have suffered a sudden catastrophic atavism. In no other manner can I account for my actions. I released her and played upon her body, which was by this time wholly available to me, like a master pianist playing upon an instrument of melodic divinity. I ran my hands lightly over her, probingly, caressingly, punctuating their avid hunt with little nips of my lips and teeth. Her form moved ceaselessly, with ever-increasing hunger. Little cries of ecstasy came from her throat and made my ego swell as had nothing ever done before.

I drew her close to me with hard strength, feeling the naked warmth of her like the radiance from a marvelous human cyclotron, penetrating me deeply with stimulating rays. Time and space ceased to have meaning. Dimensions shrank, objects were as nothing. Miss Cannon then seemed to go into a sort of trance but I became frightened. I say frightened, being kind to myself, using the euphemism. Actually I was in a blue funk. I was routed, hysterical. I leaped to my feet with a tremendous lunge that strained every muscle in my body and dashed through the door with such speed that I fell headlong down the stairs—where I'm certain I should have dashed out my brains on the tile landing had not some kind person interposed himself and stayed my fall.

"Hey," he said, "where are you going so fast?"

In my mad effort to reach what in my mind at that precise moment constituted safety, I broke away from him and dashed through the door of the building. As I tried to make my turn to head down the street, a perilous maneuver at such a speed, my shoe encountered some lubricous substance, possibly an orange ring or banana skin, and I fell resoundingly to the pavement, striking my head with stunning force.

CHAPTER TWO

LESSON ONE

WHEN I awoke I was seated in an automobile. A lanky, cadaverous individual was plying a handkerchief that had been soaked in water. "Where am I...how..?"

"You are now," said the man didactically, "seated in my automobile." I subsequently learned that he loved the sound of his voice. "You are in the twenty-six hundred block of St. Charles Street, New Orleans. You just took a dive down a long flight of steps and I was there to keep you from braining yourself on the landing. As to who you are or what, I can only go by your driver's license, which says that you are a professor of psychology at the University and your name appears to be Thomas McBride Tallant. What are your particular talents?"

I breathed deeply, and felt of the expanding hematoma on the back of my head. "It would appear that I have rather an excellent talent for getting into deplorable situations."

"Have a drink," said the affable man, handing me a flask. I handed it back with a glance calculated to indicate disapproval.

"I do not indulge in strong drink." I said stiffly.

"That so?" he said skeptically. "Well, brother, I'd surely like to know the brand of mouthwash you use. From here it smells like pure Gibson's Square Face."

"I'm not acquainted with the mouth wash," I retorted, "and for your information I have been drinking a concoction the last name of which is Collins."

"Indubitably," said the man, "I also have a weakness for a Collins when I'm thirsty, also divers other refreshing concoctions know as Planter's Punch, Manhattans, and Dry Martinis."

"I am not acquainted with them. You have been very kind and now if..." I essayed to climb from the automobile and was assailed with a qualm of nausea and weakness making it necessary to sit back and try to regain my balance and well being.

"Son," said the kind man, paternally, "you shouldn't be walking tonight after that crack on the head. Where do you live?"

"On State Street." I gave him the number and leaned my head back against the seat. "You have been most kind. Might I inquire as to your name?"

"You may. Eugene Danglos, investigator extraordinary. When I first met you I was doing a little snooping and we collided. Your speed and anxiety to vacate that house was not because of a murder by any chance?" I could feel my face reddening.

"Neither by chance nor intent," I assured him with heat. "I am not a murderer."

"You don't fly well, either," he said, with an attempt at levity which left me chill. "What were you running from?"

"That I am not at liberty to reveal. Sufficient to say it was a situation I had never before experienced." This utterance sounded a little stupid but I was afraid if I tried to correct it I'd make it worse. Moreover, this man Danglos impressed me as being abnormally acute. He might also have read Freud and shared Miss Cannon's opinion of the *lapsus linguae*.

"Did it," he inquired with a puckish glance, "have anything to do with your unzipped pants?"

In the frenzied effort to refasten them I moved too rapidly and again a feeling of nausea swept over me. I was miserable. I had been caught in a series of circumstances that the veriest moron would have interpreted correctly. I was sick and in pain. I felt like a fool. I had been beaten, first by one of my students, then by the sidewalk, and now by this sharp-eyed devil of a detective.

"That's right," he said gently, patting me on the back. "Being a detective has its compensations and although you'd have a pretty hard time telling me what happened I think I can figure it out."

"Please don't," I sobbed. "I have had more than mortal man can endure for one night and if my Aunt Cam hears about this..." That was enough of a thought to stop my sobs and straighten me up. Aunt Cam is a grenadier of a woman weighing some one hundred and seventy pounds, with hennaed hair and the constitution of a rhinoceros. She smokes frightfully long cigarettes, which she has made to order, and is never without a brooch which contains the largest diamond I ever saw. It was stolen once and the man who found it is little less than a god to Aunt Cam—short for Camilla. Aunt Cam's house sits back from the street amid tremendous live oaks and every sort of shrub you ever heard of. Squatting, as it were, in the bushes, but definitely not hiding. The house wouldn't hide any more than Aunt Cam would, and always gives the impression of being ready to spring, also a quality of my aunt. It has leaded glass windows and stately columns not unlike many houses in the district, yet with a personality all its own. Though it is said to be hundreds of years old I more than suspect it had to wait for Aunt Cam to acquire its present personality.

Mr. Danglos pulled up in front of the house and peered at it for a moment. "Then you must be Mrs. Camilla McBride's nephew?"

"Yes. How did you know?"

"I found a brooch for her. She's a character; but she never impressed me as one who would raise hell if you went on a toot."

"That is not the problem," I said shortly. "In fact, I rather suspect she'd be overjoyed, but it is a satisfaction I don't intend that she have."

This did not seem to please Danglos. "In other words you're willing to be completely dishonest about tonight, is that right?"

I flushed, my face becoming uncomfortably warm, as it always does when my blood rises.

"You haven't the remotest idea of what happened to me," I said defensively, and turned to open the heavy cast-iron gate. We passed through the gate and up the walk, I, somewhat unsteadily.

"Would you like me to paint you a picture? Well, there's a certain girl who ..."

"If you please," I hastened to interrupt. "I retract my statement. I must plead extenuating circumstances. I ... that is ... things were arraigned against me and I'm afraid ...."

"You're afraid you acted like a man, is that it? That's what your aunt probably would like to see you do. Not go off the deep end and make an ass of yourself but get around and learn to live. She told me about you. She said your two maiden aunts inhibited practically every human reaction you had; but me being what I am, and you what you are, we both know that you can't ever drive out human feeling if it was ever there. We know that it stays back in the subconscious and the unconscious to make trouble ... don't we?"

"I'm not well," I complained, "and I don't feel like talking shop. You have been kind and I appreciate it but will you please go now?"

We were on the porch and, as I had feared, the door opened. Aunt Cam stuck out her red head, all knotted up with curlers, her eyes bright and sharp.

"Why it's Mr. Danglos ... I do declare, where did you find Tom? At the library? That's where he does his dissipating. Come in, come in and have a drink. I was just about to indulge in a nightcap."

She led the way into the high-ceiled living room with its ancient weighty furniture, gilt mirrors, and handpainted table lamps.

Pleading fatigue, I excused myself, and walked with such deliberate steadiness to the staircase that Aunt Cam blared at me, "Watch your step, Junior, or you'll break your neck on those stairs."

I checked a retort and made my way carefully to my room in the upstairs south wing, where I divested myself of my clothes and turning out the light, went to bed. I tossed fitfully with innumerable half-thoughts chasing each other through my troubled mind when of a sudden I realized that on the morrow I would meet Miss Cannon again in my class. This was of sufficient shock to bring me upright in bed, dizzy and sweating. The thought of having to face her was more than I could endure and immediately I set about to plan ways and means to avoid the meeting. I would malinger ... that's it! I would be ill and I would have Josy, the colored maid, who seemed to have formed an attraction to me, call the head of the department and tell him I was indisposed. I lay back and went to sleep with little more ado.

CHAPTER THREE
HOME WORK

Josy brought my coffee the next morning and aroused me from a sleep that had been anything but restful. Miss Cannon had occupied my dreams to a considerable degree and I recalled having to wipe the perspiration from my body several times during the night.

As was her wont, Josy placed the tray strategically and proceeded to lecture me regarding my way of life.

"You ain't livin' a nachal life," she scolded vehemently. "You reads too many books when you ought to be gettin' out more." She picked up a book on psychiatry and shook it at me. "See ... see what I mean." While trying to think of means to escape from her advice and terrifying lack of delicacy, I found myself staring at the neck of her dress as it gaped in protest against the heavy bounty of a pair of breasts that were heavier and more conical than Miss Cannon's, in fact resembled them little in detail, and were yet wholly attractive nonetheless. I became lost in the delight of my observation as I had on previous occasions and when again I looked at her face it wore an all-knowing smile. "One thing," she said laughing at my discomfiture, "it sure is there. Maybe you keeps it all locked up inside you like a lot of men but it sure is there."

"I have no idea to what you are referring," I said coldly. "Would you do me a favor this morning?"

"Morning, noon, or night," she replied with too much alacrity and emphasis.

"I appreciate your kindness," I said with dignity. "I would be favored if you would call Dr. Crosby at the University and tell him that I am indisposed this morning. Nothing serious tell him. A temporary bout of malaise, a cold … tell him anything that you deem fitting. Anything of a temporary nature."

"I'll tell him," she said, "but it ain't temporary."

"What do you mean?"

She smiled slowly and walked out, her fundamental endowments moving with provocative and more than necessary animation. The impression was one of seductive insolence that I must admit made an impression, one which appalled me. Again I found myself reacting to a stimulus that I could not control nor hinder. It was most upsetting. Josy had, heretofore, been merely a servant and a fixture, nothing more. But as she went through the door I could see that she was also a healthy animal with a considerable quantity of good solid flesh arranged in a most disconcerting manner, of which fact she took the fullest advantage.

I lay back in bed and endeavored to align my mind in something resembling order but I might as well have saved myself the effort. Where there had only been Miss Cannon there was now Josy also, and between the two of them I was soon in a state of torture.

I arose and donned my clothes, having a rather astounding appetite, torture or no, something I had not experienced since my days in the service. There was also an inexplicable feeling of lightness and well being that persisted in spite of my mental turmoil, and speaking of my mind, I noticed that fleshly things seemed to have taken it over completely, without my bidding, and in spite of all my efforts. Soon I sat at breakfast with Aunt Cam, whose head was still bristling with curlers, conscious of an exuberance that I had no right to feel.

I have no conscious recollection of just how that day passed with the exception of the hour I spent in Danglos' office. In the middle of the afternoon, feeling explosive and about to burst a blood vessel or something, I went to the phone, and after some search in the directory dialed a number.

"Start talkin'!" said the voice at the other end, with such vehement bluntness that for a moment I could only gasp.

"Er ... is this Mr. Danglos?"

"Only by hearsay."

"Mr. Danglos," I interrupted with acerbity, "I do not feel equal to your badinage this afternoon. I—ah—wish to consult with you on a matter."

"Dear me, why of course," he replied, his voice chaffing in tenor. "At the moment I am unbusy, having only just handed back the Green Hornet his buzz and stinger which I used with great honor while he was on a vacation."

"I haven't the remotest idea what you mean," I said haughtily. "May I or may I not see you?"

"Oh, by all means and I'll have some Collins made up for when you get here."

"Good. I am somewhat unstrung and a few Collins might prove stabilizing."

"I wish to thank you," I said, taking the chair offered me by Danglos and sweeping his luxurious office with an appreciative eye, "for your assistance last night and accepting the blame for the smell of gin in the air. I surreptitiously sniffed a bottle of lemon flavoring in the kitchen today and found that it is within the realm of possibility that oil of lemon peel might simulate the odor of gin though, I must admit, I have never smelled gin. I am merely judging from the sound of the name."

"I can believe that," he declared solemnly. "Now smell this Collins which I have carefully prepared for you and I think you will see that the resemblance is remarkable. In fact, to make it more certain I shall put in several drops of gin, then take a sniff and you'll see."

"A few drops only," I warned. "I am most belligerently averse to the use of intoxicants."

"I'll count 'em," he promised. He did so, then handed the drink to me. He was correct. It had a very close resemblance to the lemon flavoring and there wasn't enough gin in it to change the taste at all. In fact, it was identical to the ones I had had the day before.

"Now that we're all bedded down comfy-like, suppose you tell me what's bothering you?"

I squirmed and sipped my Collins. It wouldn't be easy to tell this man with all his apparent flintiness. "Well…"

"Let me tell you. Last night you got bowled over by something you have been thinking was completely foreign to your make-up. Right there you made your first mistake, and for you, of all people, to make it is even more surprising. What does Freud say are the two most powerful drives of the human?"

"Er…um." I swallowed hard.

"All right goddammit, I'm not going to say it for you."

I held up my chin. "Very well, sex and self-preservation, the last of course embracing great numbers of…"

"Not a bit more than the first," he interrupted. "They both embrace a hell of a lot of territory. You've known that for lo these many years, and yet you've somehow managed to make something outlandish of Tom Tallant. Something not of this earth; something above all the petty reactions of man, above man as a biped, viviparous, omnivorous mammal. Now Snow White, tell me something…why?"

I took a sip from my Collins, gaining time to frame an adequate answer, but it did no good. "You see…my aunts…"

"Your aunts, my eye. All the education you have should have boiled that muck out of you years ago. Who were your aunts…God? In the last twenty-four hours you've seen all they taught you skid by the ways and yet you can't admit it. Again, why? Are you afraid? No, I take that back. Of course, you're afraid. There's no other explanation for it."

"I am not afraid," I said stoutly. "I'm merely confused, and..."

"Scared to death," he finished. "Last night, brother, if all the banshees of hell had been grasping your coat tails at every jump, you couldn't have been any more so. Your eyes were out on stems and your knees came up past your ears at every jump. You probably think you slipped on a banana peel and fell on the sidewalk. You didn't, you simply went around a corner so fast that your feet and centrifugal force couldn't make a compromise and the inevitable happened."

"You seem to know so many things," I said. "For instance, I have the uncomfortable conviction that you could teach my class so much better than I, because you know so much more of life... the life I have passed by. I am beginning to wonder if I was right."

"What you choose to call high thought is fine, Tommy, but when it shoves practical considerations out of the window, then it becomes a vice. Life, in spite of what lotus eaters and utopianists would have it, is a complicated thing the way it's set up. To have any worthwhile understanding of it takes time. Time and the same cold, critical approach with which you'd carry on a biological experiment. This is necessary so that when something comes up like last night, you can recognize it even if you can't be calm and detached about it. Some never get a working knowledge of it and there are all degrees of it more or less. You, for instance, are not what you think you are, and thereby hangs the trouble." I snapped erect at this and I must have turned the color of an impassioned turkey. "That bit you where you live," he said dryly. "Want to tell me about it?"

I shook my head. "No...that is, it's..." I waved a despairing hand and subsided. My Collins had had some effect but I felt despondent and miserable.

"Your background, Tom, has become all cluttered up with fears. Fears of every imaginable sort. I can't locate and slay each separate one for you, so we'll start at what seems to be closest to you at the moment. Heretofore, what has a woman's body meant to you?"

"Something upon which to perch a head," I said without hesitation.

"And now you find that it is quite something else…am I right?"

He was and I so indicated by a nod.

"Very well, there can be but one answer as to why a woman's body is beautiful; to attract. It does attract and more often than not the male is caught in the attraction. Years ago, some people got together and decided that this was wrong and since their word was only the word of man, they went on a little further and put out that God was the original author. All I've got to say is…it's a possibility. My personal morals needn't enter the picture because they're my own private property just as yours are your property. The moral end of the question is one for you to decide, but as you're a psychologist I needn't tell you how amenable to moral suasion your body's going to be."

Although I couldn't piece it all together into a whole, Danglos' words seemed so clear as to make me feel juvenile and ashamed. That I must seem as transparent as a third-grader was obvious and I knew that this view of me was, in one case at least, shared by my students. I shivered and felt small and inconsequential.

Danglos, as usual, divined what was on my mind. "It takes a great deal more strength to be the true Tom Tallant than it does to be Thomas McBride Tallant, the glassy-smooth psychologist who is trembling behind the glass. It takes self-searching, brutal self-analysis, and a desire for truth which transcends even the various compensatory drives that so often blind us in order to make us seem something we are not. That's what I mean when I said I have made peace with myself. I have learned that I can expect almost anything from Danglos; therefore, when it happens I'm not shocked or surprised. Danglos is part dog, part swine, part buccaneer, part cavalier, and if one looked long enough one might find an infinitesimal part of an angel. I know all that and none of the parts is likely to catch me off guard. The only way to maintain an effective guard is to know what to expect, then measures can be taken."

"You make the most crystal-clear sense I have ever heard, Danglos," I remarked, draining my Collins.

"That is the greatest compliment you could pay me," he said, "other than to remark on my good looks."

CHAPTER FOUR

LESSON TWO

ALTHOUGH it is a deucedly long way from the Pere Marquette Building to State Street, I walked it and arrived just in time for dinner, tired and sweaty, but feeling somewhat triumphant. Just why I felt this way I do not know because all Danglos had done was paint a picture for me that was stupefying. The task that lay before me was something from which my mind recoiled as it amounted to the making over of an individual. I knew what it would mean and as I was not sure of just what sort of a person this Thomas McBride Tallant fellow was, I felt futile and fearful. Josy met me at the door and solicitously took my hat, something she is accustomed to doing only for visitors.

"Dinner in 'bout fifteen minutes," she said.

"Do you know how to fix a Collins?" I asked. I felt winded and a Collins seemed immensely attractive to me at the moment.

"You means a Tom Collins?"

"Yes ... I believe that is the full name of the drink."

"Sho does. I makes a good one. I uses plenty of lemon peel oil."

"Yes, do. Make it double as I'm very thirsty and hot."

At dinner that night there was roast beef, in the cooking of which Amanda excels, and baked potatoes, rice and gravy, cauliflower, green beans and candied yams. In all, it was a delicious meal and I never recall eating with such gusto.

"You," observed Aunt Cam in her disconcerting way, "have disinterred an appetite."

"I'm feeling in the pink," I averred, taking my third slab of roast beef although it was noticeably rare. I had been trained to avoid underdone meat as an indication of savagery. Tonight I felt that I would have liked to hunt an animal, stalk it, kill it with a spear and then eat it raw. The red meat gave me the illusion of being a rough and ready man of the hunt who scorned effete cookery. After supper when Aunt Cam repaired to the library for coffee and brandy, I asked if I might have another Collins. She agreed—too readily it seemed—and summoned Josy to prepare it.

"I find it odd," I exclaimed as I tasted the Collins, "that I was never introduced to this excellent drink before. It is delicious, cool, invigorating, and seems to lift the spirits."

"Oh … yes!" said Aunt Cam hesitantly, appearing to stifle a smile. "It is most invigorating, but there's too much of it for an old woman like me."

"That's what you should be drinking," I chided, "instead of alcohol. With a Collins available, I cannot see why people will drink intoxicants."

After a period during which she seemed to strangle, Aunt Cam said, "There's no accounting for what people will do, son."

I subscribed wholeheartedly to this and sat back to drink and reflect. By nine o'clock, with my dinner and three tall Collins keeping friendly company, I was ready for bed.

"I think I shall retire," I announced. Aunt Cam nodded and placed a finger in her book as she raised her cheek for me to kiss.

"Good night, son," she said in a kind voice.

"Good night," I replied and walked from the library into the dim hall.

A hand reached out and caught my sleeve as I walked toward the stairway, startling me somewhat.

"Come on down here, Mr. Tom, I got somethin' to show you."
Josy held on to my arm as she piloted me back toward the kitchen
and down the stairs to the basement, my fears mounting as we
proceeded. I could smell her warm, clean body, slightly scented
with some kind of toilet soap, meaning that she had just bathed.
Her hair, very soft and long, was still damp around the edges. She
wore a dress that did not come together very well at the neck, and
I could see the basic swells of her fine breasts. I noted that they
were firmer than I had thought and even without their support
they stood out, the motion of her walk transmitting a certain
subtle movement to them that sent chills winging through me.

She stopped before a door. "You know what this room is?"

I shook my head. "It's my room," she said.

"But … er, ah, why did you bring me down here?"

"To show you the way."

"But why should I want to know the way?"

A slow smile spread over her face. "It might be a good thing
to know, sometime."

She opened the door and I could see a well lighted, spacious
room that was tastefully decorated, clean and cheerful. She
stepped inside and with a single movement stripped the robe
from her. The shock was such that for a moment I could only
stare at her, but I must admit, she made a striking figure.

Josy is tall, her legs are long and well formed, and they go
well with her plentiful buttocks, her magnificent breasts, and her
small waist. As soon as I could get my breath and senses, I turned
about and fled back up the stairs as fast as I could go. I didn't
stop till I was safe in my own bedroom with the door closed.
For five minutes I fought for breath and control, having been
completely unnerved by the sight, in need of a Collins as never
before in my life. Those strange impulses, urges, and emotions
were beating me to pieces. I put on my bathrobe, after a shower,
to cover my nakedness of which I was now so acutely conscious
that it amounted to physical pain. I didn't don pajamas because

I was hot as though in a fever and I felt that the robe being loose and thin would be cooler. Hearing the clink of a decanter in the library was an auditory feat, but I accomplished it. I mention it to show how keenly my senses were tuned and also because it gave me an idea. I stood by the bed for a moment, marshalling my courage, then marched out into the hall, down the steps and into the library.

"I feel," I announced somewhat lamely, "that another Collins would facilitate a good night's sleep."

"I take that to mean you feel a Collins would make you sleep better?" rasped my aunt, peering at me over her spectacles.

"That was what I was trying to project," I replied. "I would not bother you except that my knowledge does not extend to the concocting of drinks."

"Your knowledge doesn't extend to much of anything," she told me unpleasantly, "but I'll concoct if you feel that you'll sleep better. You look like you need something as a lifter. You appear to have suffered an attack of chartreuse vampire bats, but knowing you, I'd say it was unlikely."

She left and came back shortly with a Collins which, from the taste, must have been virtually pure oil of lemon peel. The results of this drink were both immediate and astounding. I felt as though I were looking at Aunt Cam from some great height and that I was capable of the most monumental feats of both physical and mental effort.

"I presume that you have been wondering what has come over me in the last twenty-four hours," I heard myself say.

"As much as I dislike shocking you, Tom, I have, contrary to your aunts' opinions, a thing in my head which passes creditably for a brain."

At the moment I was prepared to agree with her except that her sudden intelligence and perception frightened me. Aunt Cam has a certain shrewd facility for keeping her thoughts to herself until it pleases her to release them. Suppose she, Danglos, Miss

Cannon, and Josy were in a conspiracy against me. The thought chilled me and stirred up a resolve that for some reason was as rapidly dissipated as had any number of others of late. I gulped the last of my Collins and held to the chair till the repercussions had subsided to a calm, smooth thunder.

"I think I shall retire."

"And I'll get to Scotland afore ye," she said in an argot which she sometimes uses when she chooses to be abstruse. "You're a good boy, Tom," she continued, rising and planting a moist kiss upon my lips. "If by the grace of Allah you ever grow out of swaddling clothes."

I resented this but she left and did not allow me to retort. In spite of my averred intention to retire, I sat for some time in the library, not thinking, but enjoying the immense feeling of well being which the last Collins had imbued me with. I tensed my muscles and, rising, walked out into the hall. I looked toward the back of the hall where steps led to the basement and the servants' quarters. When I stopped it was before Josy's door. I was appalled for a moment but before the effect was fully felt, the door opened and there stood Josy dressed in a night garment which was so thin as to make it a negligible. She caught my hand and leading me into the room, closed the door and locked it.

"I knew you'd come back," she said standing back and arching her back, making her breasts stand out unbelievably.

"That is not possible," I retorted with some heat. "I did not know myself till a moment ago."

"I didn't say you knew it. I said I knew it."

I was impelled to touch one of her bare arms and did so without thinking. Her flesh was as firm as the meat of of a ripe fruit and the skin smooth and cool.

She looked at me with bold slumberous eyes and said, "What did you come for?"

"I do not know," I answered truthfully, reeling a little from the shock of the question. I had not been prepared for it.

"S'pose I tole you, I know why you came down here?" There was a softness in her voice that affected me strangely, a note I recalled hearing in Miss Cannon's the night before.

"I'd say you are an amazingly intelligent girl. Why did I come?" When, I asked myself bitterly, would I stop putting myself in such positions with my unguarded tongue?

However, Josy is a kindly person and only smiled. "I won't tell you, I'll show you. We jes's well set down."

She pointed to a small but comfortable divan which occupied part of one side of her room. I sat upon it, splintering waves of shock traveling over me as I observed the rich flesh of her firm thighs sliding beneath the web-thin garment. I sat without being able to take my eyes from her.

"Now you know how come you're here?"

"Er … no." This time I was less truthful as I was discovering belatedly that basic man is an entity all to itself and under the proper provocation will produce manifestations. It was, in a few moments, to take me over entirely for I'm positive I would never have so conducted myself from purely conscious intention.

Josy pulled the neck of my robe open. She put her hand therein, eliciting a sudden storm of sensation that started a dewing sweat on my forehead and increased my respiration to an alarming rate. She stroked my chest and neck, letting her hand travel to the back of my left ear where the sensation seemed to be of the highest and demanded some move from myself. Clumsily I reached over, clutched her shoulder and put forth a degree of pressure which I'm sure could not possibly have accounted for the net result. Hardly had my hand touched her when with a single movement she came over and lay against me, giving the impression that I had pulled her over. The warmth of her body was such a stimulus that I sank my hand into her back with enough force to have hurt but she only closed her eyes and made a faint throaty sound, parting her lips and forcing her face into the curve formed by my neck and shoulder. I sought to use both arms to bring her closer, an endeavor at which she was of considerable aid. In the activity I noticed that one of her long luscious legs had escaped from its frail covering and trembled nervously, the long fine muscles striated and tense. It happened then as it had happened before save that in the place of the freezing fear there was a kind of ineffable relief, a lassitude that seemed to pervade every nerve and muscle...

CHAPTER FIVE
MORE HOME WORK

I WAS awakened by a hand shaking my shoulder.

"You better get up and roll around in your own bed for a while."

I sat up dizzily and sprang from the bed. I was totally conscious, my mind clear and fully active. With frenzied haste, I drew on my robe to cover my shame, wondering how I had come here, yet retaining enough of last night to know that it had been no accident and that I was the principal culprit.

"I'm very sorry to thus compromise you, Josy. I shall leave at once and in great stealth, nor shall I trouble you again."

She smiled and stretched like a cat, throwing her breasts into vivid relief. This caused a knot to form in my throat which I resented intensely. "You'll be back," she said comfortably.

"I'll be no such thing," I countered with unwonted harshness. "I can't imagine why I came last night."

I knew I was being churlish. Actually I was hopelessly grateful to her—but too embarrassed to tell her.

I whirled and went through the door, closing it softly behind me. I made my way, as quietly as a mouse, to my own room where I proceeded to climb into my bed to give it the verisimilitude of having been slept in. As it was, I lay still a little too long and went to sleep again, being waked by Josy bringing coffee.

"Good mornin'!" she greeted me as though nothing had happened, although I could see she wore a species of smile which women in possession of esoteric secrets are often wont to wear.

I avoided her eyes and took the coffee, feeling an unaccustomed thirst which I deduced was a result of my long walk from Danglos' office the day before.

After another breakfast which made Aunt Cam's eyes gleam, I started for the University, feeling considerably better than I had in a long time. I felt cleansed, relieved, and uplifted, none of which I had any right to feel what with my recent activities. I attempted to castigate myself and logically point out that I had been a swine, a dog, everything despicable that I could lay my tongue to, when suddenly I realized that Danglos had said all those things about himself as being true, but was not the least put out about it. This threw me into further confusion which only one thing was able to dissipate. That was the sight of Miss Cannon coming into the afternoon class and of a sudden I realized that I had miscalculated. She only had classes with me on Monday, Wednesday, and Friday. I had missed Thursday which was the day she also missed and with a sudden feeling of despair, I sat down and began to call roll.

I remember very little about the lecture that day as you might be able to understand. When the class was excused, I repaired to the cloak room to make certain that Miss Cannon would leave and cause me no further embarrassment. After five minutes, I opened the door and took a quick glance at the room. It was, as I had prayed, empty, but again my lack of preparation for life was borne upon me for as I came out into the room there she stood by the blackboard which had been out of my line of vision.

"Hi, Prof!" she greeted.

"Good afternoon, Miss Cannon," I twittered weakly. "Was there something I could do for you?"

She was dressed in a cool cotton frock, not fitting like the sweater and skirt had, but well enough in its own way to cause a man's mind to veer crazily.

She nodded and pointed to the board where she had made an inscription in chalk. I read as follows: "I, Thomas McBride Tallant, do hereby avow myself as vanquished by one, Joan Elizabeth Cannon, under the conditions agreed upon and freely admit that I was wrong on all counts as described by Miss Cannon. I further agree, and admit, that in practical matters, Miss Cannon is my superior on psychological points in regard to human relations. Signed ..." There was no signature.

"You may sign this release, Prof."

"I shall do no such silly thing!" I said, my face feeling as hot as a coal grate in full operation.

"Then you don't admit it?"

"Miss Cannon, you ... That is, what happened night before last can in no way be classed as conclusive ...."

Her eyes darkened dangerously. "I think it is the very best evidence available and if you don't sign it and admit to me that you were thoroughly put in your place, I shall see that some highly embarrassing things appear on this board from time to time. Sign it now and play the game like a right guy and I'll rub it out."

There was no alternative, so I signed.

"Now," she said as she erased the statement, "do you freely and of your own will, admit that I was right and you were wrong?"

I sighed heavily and sat at my desk. "It would appear, Miss Cannon, that you are right and I'm wrong. Of one thing, I am certain. I am not the man I thought I was."

She smiled and picked up her books. "You're twice the man I thought you were, although I must admit that your precipitous exit was hardly complimentary." With that she left me alone to think dark thoughts and wonder about myself.

In the weeks that followed—it had been early September when Miss Cannon had so upset my even tenor of life—I was left to my own devices and began to feel that I was on the upgrade again, back to what, in my case, was normal. Miss Cannon left me severely alone, a matter which, I reluctantly admit, piqued me no little. Josy was her usual, affable self with never a demand or suggestion that might be classified as provocative save for the light in her eyes which I took care not to meet.

One evening after dinner, the phone rang and Josy answered.

"It's a man wants to talk to you," she said to me.

I left the library where I had been sitting with Aunt Cam who had become somewhat short with me of late, and went into the hall.

"Is that Thomas McBride Tallant?" asked the voice, which I knew at once belonged to Danglos.

"It is," I said.

"How in hell do you know?"

"It is a matter of record," I got out finally, thinking that this would stop him for good and all. It didn't.

"Have you seen the record?"

"Well … no, not exactly …"

"There y'are," he brayed triumphantly. "Someone told you there's a record and you took his word for it. What a scientist you are. However, if you are under the impression that you are Tallant, maybe you are."

"I cannot see," I said with acerbity, "why, whenever we chance to speak, we always get off at this tangent relative to our respective identities. What exactly was your purpose in calling me?"

"You kill me," he snarled. "What are you doing tonight?"

"Nothing. It is Friday night and I have no Saturday classes." Again, I burned my bridges, all of which I could have used when he next spoke.

"Good!" he said enthusiastically. "I'll be by in an hour. In that time you'll get yourself arrayed in some of your best informal finery and you and I will do a little pub crawling. It'll be good for your soul."

"My soul…" I began, but never finished. He had broken the connection.

"Who was that?" asked Aunt Cam as I walked back into the library, my brow furrowed by trouble.

"Danglos. He wants me to go with him some place and he didn't give me a chance to refuse."

"Good. You could be in no better company. You'll learn more by going out with him than you will reading that old … whatever his name is."

"Cottrell, an excellent monograph on the unconscious."

"You," she said with unclothed malice, "should have written it. Dress and go wherever Danglos chooses to take you."

I dressed in a well fitting, double-breasted tropical worsted, dark blue with a pale pin-stripe. After a look in the mirror, I decided that, all in all, it was most becoming, if not festive, attire. I discarded my glasses as I use them only for close work or reading. I combed my hair which, as usual, demanded its own way, standing up on my head in a perfect lather of duck tails as I have heard curls disparagingly called. With a final pat here and there, I went down the stairs just in time to see Aunt Cam admit Danglos, who was clad in a suit of baggy tweeds worn with a certain devil-may-care attitude which made me feel dowdy.

To my intense amazement, he bent over from his improbable height and bussed Aunt Cam heartily on the lips. This seemed to me to be the acme of insolence, but she giggled like a school-girl and slapped him playfully on the cheek.

"Oh—you devil, come on in and get the scent of that cheap whiskey off your breath."

Danglos swept her a low bow which seemed to defy the laws of gravity and said, "Just be careful that your brooch isn't missing, after I leave."

So, with such banter, they passed me standing on the stairs, stricken with astonishment, and went on into the library. The clink of glasses came to me and a toast which from Aunt Cam's laugh must have been slightly risqué. I went on in and took a seat opposite them, holding my hat in my hand.

"We won't need that," he assured me, taking it from me and sailing it across the room with deadly accuracy, hooked it neatly on the old walnut hatrack that stood near the living room door. "Where we're going, a hat is merely another thing to cost you money. You have money, I take it?"

"I have three dollars and twenty-nine cents," I said. "It should be sufficient."

"Once maybe... I can't remember when, but I say maybe because I'm naturally a careful man, but not now. Auntie, can't you furnish this lad's exchequer with a little padding? I'm sure he'll pay it back when he clips another coupon."

Aunt Cam lifted her skirt, to my horror, and skidding her stocking down a few inches, withdrew a fifty-dollar bill. "That'll be enough to take you halfway, at least," she said as casually as though drawing fifty dollars from one's stocking was an every-day occasion. "Danglos will stake you from there on."

I took the bill gingerly. "There'll be no occasion," I assured her firmly. "I cannot imagine what I could do in one night that would demand such an expenditure."

"The things you can't imagine would fill the Library of Congress," said Danglos with what I considered unnecessary brutality, but it was just his way. He is, in reality, the kindest of men though I knew him a long time before I was cognizant of the fact. We left presently, after Danglos had consumed what seemed to be enough whiskey to lay the average man flat on his back. It put him in fine fettle and when Danglos is in fine fettle he is the most garrulous person one can imagine. We climbed into his rather disreputable but mechanically excellent car, and drove off down the street.

"Now, Junior," he began, unconsciously using Aunt Cam's term of disparagement, "I shall begin by stripping you of whatever protective vestments you have been able to amass during your absence from my protective influence. You're a goddam sissy, Tommy, a bleating, whining, little pipsqueak of a sissy or you'd have been well on the way to liberation. Instead, you've crawled back into that shell, breathing rarefied atmosphere again."

"I don't suppose it ever occurred to you," I protested with considerable vehemence, "that I might like the atmosphere which you so bitterly castigate."

"Dryin' up on me, eh? Well, it harpoons you right in your tracks, don't it? No matter and maybe I'm a dunce for wasting my time on you but I hate to see a fine piece of human animal go to husk and seed without even lifting a finger."

"I'm afraid I'm not much of a subject for your treatment," I said with unaccustomed humility, for before this superbly masculine creature I did feel ashamed of myself because what he said was nothing but the unalloyed truth.

"Sweet mama!" he moaned. "I can stand anything but self-pity. On one occasion, Tom, you've seen that you have all the reactions of a man. Hell, I'm not telling you to go out and climb everything you see because for one thing you'd get your neck broken before you got far and for another it ain't good policy. But you're not making any effort at all. You haven't learned your lesson. That's where my beef is … Oh, here we are." Where we were was on a dimly lit street of the most unprepossessing character and the only doorway I could see was even more so. We parked nearby and went in, the sharp contrast almost taking my breath away. Inside, all was positively opulent. A long bar, I believe that's what they're called, ran along one wall and along the other was a row of booths. There was a considerable distance between, filled with tables, and at the far end of the room was a small dance floor behind which rose a place for an orchestra on a little dais.

All in all the place was designed to assure a feeling of luxurious ease and relaxation and I must say it achieved its aim admirably. With something akin to relief I sat on a stool at the bar, Danglos taking the one next to me.

The bartender came up exuding comradeship with good will. "What'll it be, gents?"

"I'll take a triple shot of Bourbon with a water chaser," said Danglos, as though he had said it many times before.

As the bartender's eyes switched to me I felt I should at least have one Collins to keep Danglos company. "I ... er, do you make a drink here known as ... I believe the name is Tom Collins?"

The bartender screwed his face up into such an effort of concentration that I feared he had never heard of the drink but presently his eyes lighted. "Y'know I had just about forgot how to make a Tom Collins," he said with the enthusiasm of a boy who had remembered where he had lost a treasured marble. "We git such few calls for 'em that I ..." He turned away and I could see his shoulders shake.

I touched Danglos on the shoulder. "That individual is a most accommodating person and I speak as a psychologist, not as a layman. He was so overjoyed at being able to remember how to concoct a Collins that he was laughing when he went to prepare it."

"Oh, Jim's the salt of the earth," said Danglos with a supplicating look at the ceiling.

I followed his gaze, expecting to see a religious painting or something else for which he had reverence, but there was only a mural depicting several indecorously clad maidens fleeing from a ... something that was half man and half beast. I shrugged, not understanding at all, and by that time the man came with our drinks.

"Tell me, my good fellow," I said, having intended asking some informed person at the first opportunity, "just what is it in oil of lemon peel that is so stimulating?" The man's jaw dropped for a moment and he held to the bar tightly. "Er ... well, to tell you the truth I don't really know."

"I am a man of science," I said, "and it is a mystery to me. After several of these drinks I feel empowered to perform herculean feats of physical endeavor and my mind seems sharpened to a tremendous degree. I shall have to pursue the matter further. There might be some tremendous discovery awaiting the man who finds the answer."

The barman appeared a little alarmed and looked at Danglos for enlightenment but my detective was watching the fleeing maidens again with a fixity of expression which outdid his previous efforts. The bartender, having other customers to serve, walked away with one more glance at me which I shall have to classify as enigmatic.

When the first Collins was about gone several men came out on the little bandstand and began to tune an assortment of instruments. This I viewed with alarm since they were not of the type to render a passable classic of Beethoven, Bach, or Tchaikowsky, and such jazz bands as I had heard were execrable. I was, however, in for something of a surprise. They played softly and sweetly and there was something in the subtlety of the melody which quite carried me away. It quickened my heartbeat, made a lump come to my throat, and unaccountably my feet began to tap out time against the rail. I ordered another Collins and Danglos ordered more whiskey.

"The music as played by those men is of a kind I've never heard before," I said, feeling lighthearted and unaccountably happy.

He nodded. "It has its points, but all it earns from the long hairs is a snort and a tilted nose."

I became offended at this end and said so. "I should think it a matter of the most abysmal indifference what people whose hair needs cutting think of it. I consider it wholly delightful."

There was a crash of glass behind the bar and I turned to see the barman doubling over with mirth. It took him all of five minutes to get his breath and even then he burst out at intervals for the space of some thirty minutes, and went so far as to give me a Collins for nothing.

"Jackson," he wheezed between paroxysms, "you're the cat's patootie."

"Tallant!" I corrected smilingly, not wishing to hurt his feelings because he was a most affable person, and accepted the drink with thanks. Danglos shuddered in silence for a while then mopped his eyes with a handkerchief.

"Are you weeping because you're afraid those maidens will be caught by that creature in the painting?"

He nodded, mopping fresh tears away. "That's it, Tom. I'm so damn scared he'll catch them that I'm bustin' out cryin'."

We were of course chaffing each other but it was great fun and I must admit that as a man with a quick whimsy I have been called a card.

The seat next to me became vacant and was immediately occupied by a morose individual who spoke snarlingly to the bartender and seemed to be angry, judging by the way he tossed his drink down. I did not like his looks so I turned my back on him to watch the orchestra trip lightly into a soft little ditty that reminded me of brooks rippling, springtime, flowers, and new-mown hay. It had a rhythm which excited my feet again and I began to strike the rail, keeping time to the tune. I felt a tap on my shoulder which might have been called a blow as it was much too sharp merely to call one's attention. I turned around to see the man next to me leaning forward, his fact twisted in rage.

"Cut out that tappin' or I'll bust you one," he growled.

I gave him a look which I strove to make cool and forbidding and deliberately turned my back on him again. Nor did I cease tapping time to the tune. Immediately I felt his hand on my shoulder and the crushing grip made me wince with pain.

"I told you to cut that tappin', bud, and I wasn't kiddin'."

"You," I said levelly as I could, "will take your hand from me instantly."

He grinned and the hand bit cruelly into the muscles of my shoulder. Danglos saw things were becoming tense and rose languidly. With my free hand I motioned him back. "I'll take care of this," I said. He stopped but he he didn't sit down.

"Okay, Tom. I'm backing you."

I faced the man again. "Apparently you are hard of hearing," I said to make sure that he had not misunderstood.

He grinned again. "Go home, pussy pants, and play with your kittens."

Seeing that remonstrance would avail me nought I resorted to a tactic which is effective but not necessarily disabling. Like a shot my hand flew out and the heel of it landed with brutal force on his Adam's apple. The shock and surprise together with no uncertain force skidded him off the stool to a ludicrous sitting position on the floor which made several onlookers roar with laughter and the bartender emit a delighted whoop of joy. The man rose from the floor fairly foaming with rage, only to be confronted by several muscular men who I was to learn are called bouncers. "Hey, fellers … just lay off a little minnit," begged the barman. "History is about to be made."

I naturally didn't know what he meant but I could easily understand the mien of the angry man when he was released. He threw a wild right at me which I caught easily, stepping back from it, and twisting it viciously. Thus I caused him to lean far over to his right which is the goal of the tactic. With his left ear thus exposed I smote him sharply beneath it with the edge of my right hand and our belligerent friend lost all interest in current matters.

The bartender looked triumphantly at the bouncers. "See what I mean. Now take that bastard and heave him onto the street and git 'im outa my sight."

"One moment," I protested. "This gentleman was perturbed and unhappy. It is possible that my foot tapping irritated him beyond endurance and at least from his own point of view he was justified in assaulting me. Let's have no further hard feelings by treating him evilly." I bent over and helped the man to his feet. "Give the man a drink on me."

My magnanimous action drew many an odd glance and oddest of all from the man whom I had smitten below the ear. He rubbed the place and sat unsteadily on the stool. After taking his drink in a shaky hand and swallowing it at a gulp he turned and considered me through feverish eyes.

"Y' know, ... you're an all-right character."

I felt warm and pleasant inside, a friend to all people. "I'm a man of science," I said. "I understand these things. I harbor ill will against no man, feeling that such low emotions are beneath my dignity."

"I'm Wallace Conway," he said with a sudden rush of feeling.

I took his hand which was large and muscular. "I am Thomas McBride Tallant, associate professor of psychology at the University."

"Pleased t' meetcha," he said. "I work sometimes, too."

We chatted pleasantly about this and that and after another drink Wallace started to leave. "You're a right guy, Prof," he said. "And you're a pal of mine."

I thanked him for his good will and watched his broad back disappear into the night.

"Say, Prof," said the barman enthusiastically, "you got a sleeveful of tricks, ain'tcha?"

"I was considered proficient at Judo during my tenure in the service," I replied modestly. "It has to do with using one's opponent's struggles and momentum to advantage. There are also certain vulnerable spots which react to specific pressure or other stimulation."

"Well," said Jim, laughing heartily, "you sure specified his stimulation for 'im." With this, many listeners burst into mirth which I joined as a point of good fellowship, not because I considered his ungrammatical sally humorous.

"Before you get the big head, son," said Danglos *sotto voce,* "just remember that you're still in swaddling clothes. What you did was muscular, not psychological."

"I made a friend of a man whom I might as easily have had as an enemy," I pointed out.

"Easier," he agreed, "but let's take another angle. See that chick sitting in the booth over there?"

I looked and averted my eyes quickly because the lady in question was staring directly at me and I was embarrassed. "Yes!" I hissed. "You should be a little more careful, though; she was looking right at me."

"Maybe she wants to dance with you."

"I am not adept at terpsichorean endeavor. As a matter of fact I have never danced in my life."

"Then how do you know you can't dance?" More of his brutal logic. "Anyone who can tap time to music with his feet can dance ... give it a try."

I considered the matter and then considered the girl as she had changed her gaze and was now looking toward the band stand. She reminded me of Miss Cannon in some ways and in others she didn't. Her face was more classic, with finer bone structure and her lips seemed thinner and more composed. She was tall and slender and wore a well fitting suit of some green material the exact nature of which I could not determine, having no knowledge of such matters. The dignified cast of her face contained a note of warning and I was afraid if I approached her I might be met with a cool rebuff, a matter of some concern to any sensitive person.

"You mean it would be socially acceptable for me to approach this young woman with a request to dance without a formal introduction?"

"By the letter of social law, no," said Danglos with a grin, "but from a purely utilitarian angle, yes."

"I'm afraid my courage is not up to the effort." I said, casting a quick glance at the lady again which caught her looking at me. I averted my eyes in confusion and directed my attention to the music, now a soft throbbing Latin melody which seemed to get into my blood. The lights of the place changed and a sort of rosy radiance came slowly into being which enhanced the attraction of the primitive rhythm. I momentarily forgot the woman in the booth and was enjoying the orchestra when I turned around to face her at a distance of no more than two feet. I was startled for a moment but a warm smile on her lips and the effects of the music combined to produce a sort of false courage which I had never exhibited before.

"Do you dance the rhumba?" she wanted to know.

I swallowed and admitted that so far as the evidence went I could not dance at all.

"This to my intense regret," I added with a touch of the cavalier.

"It is of no importance," she said. "I could teach you in a matter of seconds."

At that moment I felt I was equal to anything and having mastered several sciences in my day I saw no reason to quail before a mere musical arrangement of pedal activities. I walked with her to the small dance floor, which boasted only two couples to interfere with us, and she instructed me in the rudiments of the rhumba.

"The steps are simple," she explained. "You count one, two, three, and the feet move with the count and the music. The basic step is a repetition of that count. One, two, three; one, two, three.... See?"

"It seems simple," I agreed, but—" I stopped. I could not ask how she managed to get such movement into her hips and the very thought made the blood rush to my face. She was evidently a very perceptive person because her silvery length sparkled and she explained.

"One simply sits down ... this way on one hip, then the other. It is not as it seems a hula effort at all, merely what happens when you sit on the hips alternately." She made several practice moves for me to watch. "Now let's try it together."

I suppose I must have put forth a goodly effort as I was warmly complimented when the music stopped by the lady, whose name I had discovered was Charles. An odd name for a lady but I did not question her as it would have been rude. Charles Kensington was the full name and of course I had in return given her mine. We went back to the booth and I waved at Danglos to come over but he declined and made a sign to me which I failed to interpret, but it seemed to be something in the nature of wishing me well.

"What would you like to drink?" I asked, feeling that it was my place to suggest a tipple if she desired one. "I never drink alcoholic beverages myself but I have no objection to others imbibing."

She looked at me a little strangely, I thought, and said she would take a Scotch and water. I summoned a waiter and ordered for her and asked him to tell Jim to make me a Collins. Again I received the enigmatic look but I let it pass, feeling much too exultant to be troubled by mere glances which I did not understand. "I find," I said, "that this drink called Collins has a fortuitous formula, devised by accident no doubt, that is no end stimulating. Having done some research on the matter, I can only attribute the circumstance to the content of oil of lemon peel. I shall pursue the matter further, for I feel that some harmless and yet powerful stimulant might be found. Think what an aid to medical science such a thing would be."

"May I pinch you?" she asked with a queer little smile.

It was a moment before I could speak. "Why ... er, why not? Especially if you make it a gentle pinch; but I must confess I fail to see ..."

"Just to make sure you're real, that's all."

"Oh, I'm real enough," I said. "I am, you know, a psychology professor."

"Yes," she said and her tone was baffling, as was the little frown in her forehead. She was silent for some time, apparently wrestling with some mental problem. At length she turned to me. "Do you have to stay here?"

"I don't know," I said dubiously. "I came with Mr. Danglos and it might be a little unseemly to leave him ...."

"If I can make it all right with him would you go with me? I want to talk to you and this atmosphere is disturbing."

Before I could answer she was on her way to the bar and as she walked I again admired the classic mould of her body and the swift grace of her stride. She came back smiling. "Mr. Danglos is agreeable. He wants me to beat some sense into your head. I'll call a taxi for you when you're ready to go home."

I said this scheme sounded quite all right and we left, Danglos dropping me a tremendous wink which for some reason made the blood rise to my face.

CHAPTER SIX

LESSON THREE

Charles' apartment was larger than Miss Cannon's and altogether different. It was, to say the least, fabulous. I had judged by her appearance and bearing that she was a woman of considerable means but when I saw her quarters I was sure of it. It was very modern with a great deal of chromium and onyx decor with softly blended colors and subdued lights, all of which gave the place a most delightful and restful air. I sank into an article of furniture which I shall call a couch but should have a more exotic name. It was unbelievably soft and so comfortable that I felt like lolling about after the fashion of a spaniel. She unbuttoned my coat and in spite of my protest pulled it off.

"It'll be more comfortable. Now what sort of drink is it you like? ... Collins, was it?"

"Yes. Can you make it?"

"I'm not sure and if you don't like it just let it sit. I'm not very good at making drinks."

In ten minutes she came back with a tray of drinks, having changed to a long garment of heavy white silk that trailed to the floor with a baffling wrap around effect that made her look even taller and its fit can only be mentioned, not described. Her slender hands came forth from the sleeves like twin orchids from a bed of snow—fragile, pink and lovely. The slight lovely olive tint of her skin was enhanced by the white of the garment. She had let her hair down and it billowed over her shoulders in a kind of orderly disarray that almost took my breath away. She put the drinks on a small glass-topped table and sat beside me, drawing her tiny feet from a pair of ridiculous fluffy mules and tucking them out of sight beneath the folds of the garment.

"How is it, Thomas," she said, handing me a Collins which seemed to be correct in every respect, "that a man in your profession apparently knows so little of the things he teaches?"

I shrugged, feeling that I could talk to her freely as she did not take the attitude that I was a three-year-old. "Life has been kept from me, rather, I from it, by a pair of maiden aunts. They died and that naturally placed me more in touch with my fellows but I'm afraid I was so conditioned to solitude and self-sufficiency that I resisted what little enlightenment came my way. It has been only recently that the full force of my ignorance has been visited upon me. There have been several regrettable incidents which I feel impelled to say had rather a crushing effect on me in a manner that tended to drive me back further into my shell."

"Yet there was another force put in motion," she said. "It impelled you in the opposite direction."

"Your surmise is correct. As Danglos so brutally put it, I'm—I'm afraid of life. Actually I'm afraid of it because I am not conditioned to it. I cannot seem to meet it on equal terms and one avoids things at which one does not excel or at least perform passably. Danglos is a very wise but a very rough man who means well but who has had no experience, apparently, with people who do not have his rugged extroverted outlook and cannot grasp courage in a horny fist and make it produce. No one realizes more than I that I am at best only part of a man. I am not even qualified to teach my class because students feel that they can expect me to slay their dragons for them whereas I can only plaster them with psychological bromides and blush if their questions approach the indelicate."

She placed a hand on one of mine, the touch being such that a lump came to my throat. "Thomas, you are, as you pointed

out, a case of underdevelopment, not because you are less intelligent or less fully endowed but because you were sheltered for
so long. There is only one way to overcome this condition and
that is by exposure and gradual growth. It will be faster in your
case because of your age, but a lot will be distorted, requiring
later assessment. Things swallowed in gulps cannot be well mas-
ticated. There will be many bumps and many disappointments
because of the standards you have set up in your mind. Ideals
must be reasonable and must allow for the human element if they
are to be applied to humans. You have me built up right now into
the form of a fine lady and I like to think that I'm a lady, that I
have taste, a sense of decorum, and am not a little tart who is out
for what she can get."

"You could never be that," I said with feeling.

"How do you know?" Her logic was beginning to resemble
Danglos'.

"Of course I don't know, but you have all the fine points
which one finds in a lady."

"I'll even grant you that, Thomas, therefore we must examine
the term 'lady'. It means something different to every person. If
you have me placed as a lady in the same sense that your two
maiden aunts were ladies, you couldn't be more wrong. I like to
think that I know how to conduct myself, but I am only human."

I pondered over this bit of saber-sharp reasoning. It appealed
to me, making me feel silly because I had not long ago recognized
that there could never be all good nor all bad any more than there
could be a condition of all hard or all soft, hot, cold... numerous
examples.

I smiled. "Then the clergy in their efforts to rout sin are up
against something bigger than they are."

"It is a part of themselves," she said, lighting a cigarette and
placing it in a thin jade holder that seemed the color of her eyes.
"The sin they rant about is as important as the good they invoke,
since in the total absence of one the other loses its meaning."

I drank in her words like a thirsty camel. "I don't think I've ever met anyone quite like you."

She smiled and made a face at me that wrinkled her nose adorably. "I said that first." She got up and, walking to a huge radio phonograph, turned a switch. Soft melody began to filter into the room. She held out her arms and sidled to me. "Let's have another lesson in the art of corn-treading."

I was nothing loath, and to hold her close and breathe the fragrance of her soft hair were enough to give wings to my feet and a lift to my heart. I must have held her tightly because she raised her head from my shoulder, her eyes devilish. "Whatever there is wrong with your background, there seems to be nothing the matter with your inner self, Thomas. Do you enjoy holding me like this?"

My voice was husky. "If I liked it more, I couldn't stand it. You're the most beautiful woman I ever saw."

She reached up and with a delightful little gesture of her hands, kissed me lightly. Lightly or not it almost floored me, and I missed a step.

"Let's sit," she said. "Dancing becomes hazardous when the man gets cross-eyed."

I laughed hollowly, my heart still thudding against my ribs in a manner which shook me. She sat quite close to me this time and as always happens under such circumstances I lost conscious control and someone else seemed to take over my actions. I even listened to myself making speeches which were foreign to me, as though I were attending a lecture. "You seem to know every-thing, Charles. Why is it that you affect me the way you do? I hurt inside, I can't seem to breathe well. I'm confused and exalted at the same time."

"The symptoms are as old as man," she said softly, her hand caressing my cheek, making me cringe from the shocking sense of utter gluttonous enjoyment. I caught the hand and kissed its small damp palm, pressing my lips hard against it, wishing I could hurt myself with it in some manner not injurious to her. When I looked at her face it was very close to me framed in its glorious dark hair. Her lips parted and her eyes glowed so softly that tears stung my eyes.

"You can stop me if you wish," I could hear myself saying, "but I cannot stop myself."

I was moving toward her as I spoke and a tender smile touched her lips. "I don't want to stop you. Remember I'm human, too."

My hands were hard on her back and I could feel the fine rippling muscles as her body reacted even as had mine. I crushed her pliant body close, her hair covering us in a smother of such ineffable delight that a noise of sheer sensuous ectasy came from my throat, making me release her lips to give it voice. She relaxed and lay back against the couch, her eyes bottomless mysteries asking, demanding, and man that I was I could not have resisted should the next moment have been my last. I made a plaything of her soft damp mouth, feeling and not feeling the impression of her sharp teeth on my nether lip and the sweetness of her lingual explorations. Breathing was a matter of such dire necessity that we halted and looked at each other. Her breath came down in quivering sobs and her eyes caressed me in a manner that I could almost feel.

"Thomas … you … you're a darling … oh, such a darling."

She leaned forward and placed her face against my chest and shuddered heavily then sat back again, a tremulous smile on her face.

"Do you like me?"

My answer was to hold her close again not in passion but in gratitude and the very deepest affection. Like a reed her slim body bent and conformed to mine as I pressed her close without being rough. I turned off all but one dim light. She sat up and came into my arms, her face wet with tears, the reason for which I could not ascertain. Her hair floated around us in tangles of web-light fragrance making a fragile tent for our faces which seemed unutterably cozy and wonderful past imagination.

Her sobbing increased in tempo as the clutch of her arms tightened and her body became a thing of the most extraordinary motion and contortion, her cries louder, then a tremendous tension, stillness... utter fainting relaxation. For a long time I held her close, feeling the tremors shake her then lessen, till finally she breathed the slow measured respiration of sleep. Never have I wanted so overpoweringly to make myself a part of another, to immerse myself in another identity. I felt as though I should like to milk her of some unguent and anoint every inch of my skin with it, to clothe myself with her body... all manner of wholly impossible things to assuage this want that ached in me like a throbbing nerve. I must have translated something of my thoughts into bodily motion because she awoke and raised her head to look at mine.

She took my head in her arms and crooned softly to me as though I were a child and I'm afraid that again I wept a little, the tears making a silver trail across one of her breasts. After a while I felt better and sat up, bringing her with me, trying to straighten the tangles from her hair with clumsy fingers. Her eyes, softly green in the dim light, regarded me gravely and with such serious steadiness that I couldn't stand it and I drew her across me, cradling her in my arms like a baby, brushing back her hair. I kissed her with all the love a man can put into such a caress and the effect left tears in her eyes which she brushed away, then she sprang from the bed and ran to her dresser where she plied a stiff brush to such good effect that her hair stood out as though electrified and covered her shoulders and neck in a smother of shining glory.

I got up and went to the dresser, burying my hands in the shimmering mass of hair with a sort of restrained hysteria, clutching it and massaging it between my hands. She gasped a little as I inadvertently pulled it and I felt like some particularly low species of dog and begged her forgiveness so abjectly that her silvery laugh came bubbling out.

"It's funny ... I only met you tonight and yet I know all about you. I've always known."

"Yes," I said softly, "you're the only one who does. Danglos knows a lot, another girl I met knows a lot, Aunt Cam knows a lot, Josy knows a lot—but you know everything. I feel that even though I know it doesn't sound reasonable. I feel the same way about you. I'm not embarrassed before you. I feel comfortable, no shyness, no restraint, no secrets, no responsibilities. As far as I'm concerned, you're the most wonderful person in the world."

She finished brushing her hair and made room for me to sit beside her on the little stool. She tossed the hair back over her shoulders and together we looked at our reflections in the mirror.

"Thomas, I think it's time you knew a few things. That drink which you guzzle by the pint is not a harmless mixture with a stimulating overdose of oil of lemon peel. It is a very good drink containing an alcoholic stimulant known as gin. I want to lay that illusion by the heels and I want a lot of others to follow it. You're a psychologist and there are a few things you must know. Face them, and become for all time what you've been here tonight. I want you to be an intelligent self-reliant man. You have all the ingredients, you know where the trouble lies, you know what to do about it ... so do it! I don't want to be ashamed of you."

I had not spoken because I was staggered. To think I had been consuming alcohol in that amount and had never been aware of it! "It does appear that Danglos could have apprised me of the alcoholic content of a Collins," I said in a wounded tone.

"He didn't because he knew you'd immediately lay off and as far as I can see they've been your salvation. Alcohol is like anything else. Good in moderation, terrible in excess. It merely brings the man to the fore and shows him up for what he is." Her tone changed. "Thomas, kiss me ...."

The dawn found us rested with sweet sleep the like of which cannot be achieved in any other way. I kissed a handy thigh making her raise her head.

"Hello!" she said, her hair tangled and her eyes heavy with sleep.

She touched my face with her delicate hands as though it were some new wonder unfolded to her, then she kissed me and slipped from the bed. She donned her robe and disappeared in the kitchen where she concocted immensely attractive smells, then in what seemed a very short time she came to the door and called me.

Souse and eggs is a dish I had never tried before but it was well worth the trial. It was delicious and I left the table feeling like I owed a heavy bill and a heavier tip. After breakfast, while she showered and dressed, I made myself comfortable in the living room with a morning paper which I had found just outside the door. I could hear her clear voice singing as she made up the beds and it soothed me like the touch of a cool hand on a hot brow. There was a page of pictures and leaping at me from one corner was Charles clad in the briefest of bathing garments standing beside a ratfaced individual for whom I conceived an instantaneous dislike. Then I read the caption. "Mr. and Mrs. Denville Chatsworth Palmar honeymooning at Miami Beach. ..." I leaped to my feet and stood swaying for a moment—then like a man possessed I fled from the room. There was no Danglos to catch me this time and, of course, this time I didn't fall because I wasn't fleeing actually. I was floating, rather, like some improbable character in a bad horror picture. I didn't know what street I was on and I didn't care so I walked and walked and kept on walking.

CHAPTER SEVEN
GIN AND BARE IT

D OCTOR CROSBY was lean and eagle-visaged and his hair stood up on his head like the bristles of a wart hog. His jaw had the cut of a destroyer and his nose could have been the ram of a Confederate ironclad. It is reputed that he not only reads minds but reads thoughts not yet fledged.

He placed his bony fingers in the accredited academic pyramid and looked severely over them. "Now, go over that again, Tallant, and slowly. I didn't get it the first time."

I shrugged wearily. "I said, sir, that I have discovered that I am not qualified to teach a class in psychology."

"Ummm…indeed? If I recall correctly your marks at Columbia were excellent. Dr. Mackinsen spoke highly of you."

"If Dr. Mackinsen thought I could teach then he was an ass." The remark was not an insult due to its entire lack of animation.

"What exactly has brought you to this conclusion?" he asked.

"Myriads of things," I replied listlessly, "I can't answer questions because all I know comes from books. I'm embarrassed when students ask them, and I half suspect that they are contemptuous of me."

"Schizoid!" muttered the doctor loud enough for me to hear it.

"Doubtless," I agreed. "Or something. But whatever it is I wish to resign."

"What does your aunt think of this—ah, drastic move?"

"It was she who suggested it, sir."

Dr. Crosby was stunned for a moment. "Suggested it? Her?"

"Yes, sir."

He lifted his shoulders a little and let them fall. "Very well, Tallant. It happens that I can replace you very handily at this time, otherwise I would be in a spot. However, there's one thing."

"Yes, sir?"

"If for one moment you think you're pulling any wool over my eyes, you're a lot worse mistaken than Mackinsen may have been about you. Right now you are practically in shock. When have you slept last?"

I lifted a hand and let it fall. "Oh ..."

"Yes!" he barked. "Doubtless! Something, my boy, has rocked you to the very core and if you think for a moment that you can beat it down to a nub all by yourself then *you're* an ass. You'll wind up in a padded cell somewhere—or the morgue. You, a man who has studied the mind, should know that. Get a confidant, it doesn't matter who, and get it off your chest. I should be glad to have you tell me but I've been in this racket too long not to size up probabilities in a hurry. You won't tell me, and even now you're wishing to hell I'd shut up and let you go."

This startled me because at that precise moment I was thinking that precise phrase. Dr. Crosby smiled.

"Denser men than you, Tallant, are just as transparent to an old horse like me. You may be relieved of your duties as of now and I'll get Wilkinson to take over your class ... and Miss Cannon."

This was another shock but I was becoming inured to them. I thanked him and walked to the door. On an impulse I turned about. "How do you know about Miss Cannon, sir?"

"Miss Cannon, Tallant, is my niece ... goodbye and come to see me any time."

I thanked him and made my way back to the building to get my effects. There was no class in the room at the time and I was glad because I wished to have no explanations to make. As usual my joy was short-lived.

Miss Cannon came in and surveyed me with hot eyes.

"So you can't take it and like the proverbial puppy you're tucking in your proverbial tail and taking a proverbial powder."

"How would you like a bust in the proverbial kisser?" I shot back at her, half blind with fury.

For a moment she regarded me with surprise, her mouth open, then she burst into peal after peal of merry laughter.

She was silent for a moment then she said in a tone I had never heard her use before, "Prof, you think I'm pretty awful, don't you?"

I suppose I was sorry for myself or maybe it was something in the quality of her voice that touched me but suddenly I had to sit down at my desk. "Miss Cannon, as far as I am concerned there is no one quite so awful as Thomas McBride Tallant. I have nothing to say of you but the best, believe me. I harbor you no ill will and one of these days I may even be tempted to kneel at your feet and kiss the hem of your dress. It is true that since my encounter with you my life has been an endless series of complexities and mishaps but that can be ascribed to my lack of the ability to cope with them rather than any act of yours."

She was very close to me and I could see from the rise and fall of her marvelous breasts that she was laboring under the stress of considerable emotion. She placed a soft hand on mine. "I'm sorry, Prof. As you say I didn't mean all this to happen. You're going to resign?"

"I already have."

"Do you have all your stuff together, Prof?"

"I … yes … nothing much here, you know. A brief case, a few books … papers."

"Okay. Come with Joan. I'm beginning treatment as of now.

I went with Miss Cannon simply because I had neither the will nor the courage to beg off. My mind just locked up on me and I was left wandering about without a brain like a victim of unsuccessful lobotomy. Soon we were sitting in Miss Cannon's car at the same drive-in where I was introduced to my first Collins. I now clutched another and proceeded to break all records drinking it. It trickled through my numbed nervous system like electricity and before the second was well on its way I began to have coherent thoughts. I felt a sudden warm regard for Miss Cannon, plucking me as she was from the depths of despair. "Miss Cannon, allow me to say that I consider you an immensely nice person."

Her eyes were roguish now. "Really—even after my fall? I should think that a man of your background would consider me a lost woman."

"I have found," I said, gazing somewhat abstractedly into the Collins, "that my background made me a misfit and with what strength I can bring to bear I am trying to battle it. Until I knew better, I did consider you a brash but not an evil person."

"And I think you have taken the first toddling steps toward real wisdom. Skoal!" She held up her glass and emptied it.

I fear that after several Collins at the drive-in and several more at Miss Cannon's apartment I was approaching what has been described as a state of intoxication. I felt bitter, miserable, garrulous and inclined to confidences. Indeed, it relieved me no end to unburden myself to Miss Cannon and I was grateful for her patient ear.

"After that night with Charles," I continued, "and all it seemed to mean to both of us, there she was in the newspaper with her husband staring at me from the left—no the right hand corner of the sheet. So again I fled. I always seem to be fleeing from something."

She sat opposite me with a drink in her hand, her legs crossed, showing a considerable area of smooth skin.

"Naturally you're always fleeing from things. Man has three choices in life. To ignore, to conquer, or to flee. You evidently have little faith in your ability to conquer, you can't ignore, therefore you flee. Simple."

I hung my head for even if there was no rebuke implied, the fact stood fast that I was a man who would rather run than fight. "But I'm not a coward," I protested. "Just the other night I overcome a belligerent man at a night club with my bare hands."

"There are," she said, carefully spacing words as though speaking to a singularly dense person, "any number of different kinds of cowardice. But I haven't said that you are a coward."

"No, you haven't. You merely showed that I'd prefer to run than to come to grips with a situation."

"Another thing, Prof. I recall a remark you once made in class and I quote. 'The hasty acceptance of a theorem or even of a hypothesis, to say nothing of a postulated fact, without first examining all available evidence as well as the manner in which this evidence has been amassed and by whom, is directly contrary to all the laws and spirit of science.' Didn't you say that?"

"I seem to recall saying something like that."

"Very well. Let us pose a problem. You saw this picture in a paper. For the sake of argument, we'll assume that in spite of the opportunities for a mistake it was in truth the same girl. Remember this girl Charles had told you nothing of her past, present, or future. As far as I can see, she owed you nothing by way of explanation because matters had not progressed so far as to make it either necessary or called for. In spite of that you bust a gasket and go tearing off without a word, without giving her a single chance to lift a hand in her own defense. From the scientific angle you said something and you weren't enough impressed by it to use it in your own behalf. In the light of plain fairness, cricket, rules of the game, and all that you kicked her over and left her where she fell. In short, Thomas McBride Tallant, you are stewing in your own juice simply because all the logic and reason you've been spouting, all this high thought and your ranting about how true justice would never achieve its rightful place without the cold unemotional hand of science, was a lot of guff that sounded most pleasant to your own ears but meant nothing to you otherwise.

I felt as if I had been beaten over every part of my body with sticks till I was numb and nerveless. I sat for some time with my head hanging, unable to make a reply. "All you say is true, Miss Cannon. Danglos says the same thing, as does my aunt. I admit it but what can I do about it?"

With one of her sudden changes of temper, Miss Cannon came over to the couch and knelt by me, forcing my head back, and with this advantage she kissed me, pressing me close with her warm body. I will say this—for or against me—no matter what pressing circumstances might be plaguing me, the touch of Miss Cannon's warm lips crushed out all other considerations and I returned her caresses with a will. With her kneeling on the couch, I was placed in a lower position, but one from which other caresses could be achieved with greater freedom and with both my hands free I soon felt her cool delightful skin come under my touch. She tore her lips from mine, hugging me hard to her breast, her breath rasping from the force of respiration while my hand sent her body into shudders. Finally we both tired of the game. I picked her up—she was no light burden I can assure you—and carried her to the bedroom.

When I got home that night I was in the sort of daze during which the mind reacts to natural stimuli but offers nothing of itself to torment or confuse. I was conscious that I staggered somewhat but it was another of those things that seemed to be of little or no importance at the time. I was burning with thirst and I thought: if only Josy were awake to make me a Collins. She was and after she let me in and assisted me to my room, she said, "You want something to drink before you goes to bed?"

I nodded dully, wishing I had the strength to thank her properly. "Yes, I could do with a Collins—at tall one. And this time put plenty of gin in it."

She took my advice literally and I took the drink down halfway in a single gulp. It made me feel better and gave me strength.

Josy assisted me to undress. I assured her it was unnecessary but she insisted on it and there was nothing I could do. That is, until she threw her arms around me. Like a dash of hot water the sensation of her smooth body shook me and the pressure of her drove all thoughts of sleep from my mind. I remember thinking even as a thunderous oblivion claimed me that every day I was learning more and more of things the existence of which I had never suspected.

Please understand about the oblivion just mentioned. What I was oblivious to included just about everything—except Josy. To her I was keenly alive, and of all her delicious parts I was most acutely aware. Though possessed of barely any experience in such matters, I needed little guidance in availing myself of the proffered fruits. Instinct, and her enthusiastic cooperation, took care of everything.

As I was to learn eventually, I was much too precipitate in pursuing my satisfactions. I hardly paused to regale myself on those sleek velvet breasts before plunging more deeply into the fleshpots. Josy giggled and encouraged and cooed, but I had a feeling, after my first explosive triumph, that she was not altogether happy with my efforts. At any rate, she signified her readiness to continue the game which I gratefully considered terminated.

Tired as I was, it was beyond me to rise to the occasion, or so I thought. Josy cheerfully and proficiently changed my mind, teaching me much in the process. She began this second round with moist, soft kisses directed first at my face, then my neck, then the reaches of my chest. While her lips continued to roam like butterflies, her caressing hands came into play. My flesh literally crawled with sensations of unprecedented delight. Soon I was responding, emulating on her own lush body the procedures she was applying to mine with lip and finger.

The effect was to galvanize her. She began to writhe and wriggle. My mouth and my palms, I must confess, were finding strange and amazing thrills lurking in the ample folds and curves boasted by my sweet Josy. Even the scent of her, akin to cinnamon, contributed to my voluptuous pleasure. When her mouth, with a daring that amazed me, pursued strange explorations, I first gasped out my ecstasy, and then, teased beyond endurance, seized her in my arms and brutally had my way with her—a development which seemed to please her mightily.

For a few moments she lay quiet and content in my arms. Then she sighed, "I just knew you had it in you." She added triumphantly, "I hardly had to teach you a thing."

"Well," said Aunt Cam at breakfast the next morning, "you're a free man now, Tom. What are your plans?"

I shrugged. "Now that I've followed your advice I don't know. If something doesn't happen pretty soon though, I..." I shook my head and tried to steady the cup of coffee that threatened to slop over.

"I never thought that a woman would bring you to this state," she said, sighing. "You who were so hard to corner, into whose life no woman need come!"

"No more did I, and of course you'll tell me that this has been said times over by every love-smitten lad who ever pined ... there's just no one like her. She's in a class all her own without a single rival and I know that this is not all her personal attraction. It is some sort of reflection of myself in her or else it is some nebulous thing that attracts me as something I've always wanted and could never identify, consequently never find ... till I met her. I'm not even me when I'm with her, I'm another man, a more complete man. I lose my fears and things complicated become simple."

"And yet you dashed out and left her without letting her even explain. There could have been an explanation, you know."

I nodded humbly. "The fact is being brought to my attention constantly."

"Well, are you going to sit there and look miserable, or are you going to do something about it?"

A chill struck me at the thought of facing Charles. Apology comes easily only to the lips of a man who is so thumpingly normal or so vaingloriously in command of himself as to put me to shame.

"You're going to have to whip it alone, son," she said. "Actually, staying here might be the worst thing for you. Why don't you get a little flat in the French Quarter and wander about down there for a while and try to pull yourself together?"

"The expense of such a program would, I fear, be prohibitive," I said, shuddering at the idea of being alone in the French Quarter.

"Never mind that," she said. "I shall order my bankers to honor your draft on my account. Just check on me as you feel necessary. You've a heavy stake in my will, you know, and you might as well get some of it, now, while you need it."

I promised to think it over and quite without knowing where I was headed, I went downtown and found myself an hour later whacking my knuckles on Danglos' office door.

"Come in," he yelled.

I went in. "Good morning," I said formally.

"Uh oh … I know that tone. What happened this time?"

"I, Mr. Danglos, am in a predicament."

"You, Mr. Tallant, have been in a predicament ever since I've known you."

"Yes, I suppose so … of one kind or another. The others were merely irritating, this one is deadly."

"Ummm … so?"

"I have resigned my post at the University."

He sat up suddenly, his shin coming in painful contact with the drawer of his desk, eliciting a harsh word. "You mean you've pulled stakes? Quit?"

"Just that. I did not consider myself a fit person to instruct others."

He nodded slowly still not understanding. "I can see how you might come to that conclusion, but why the sudden decision?"

"Do you recall the lady with whom I danced the night you took me with you to Slim Jim's?"

His lips pursed. "I recall her well because she was a chick of the sort one does not find in superfluous numbers. What does she have to do with it?"

I told him the story, in greater detail and with a great deal more force than I had intended, but when I started I became excited and the relief in telling him was so great that I did an excellent job of it.

Danglos lit a cigarette and sat looking at it for some time as though the smoke might offer a solution.

"You were taken there by taxi from Slim Jim's, weren't you?"

"Yes ... it was a Yellow." Hope flowed through my veins and I managed to withstand a scorching look he gave me.

"I'm glad you remembered something." He dialed a number, "Jack, this is Danglos ... yeah. Look, a hack of yours picked up a couple at Slim Jim's on ... oh, let me see. Yeah, October the second at two minutes to eleven. A man and a woman, think you could check that for me? I want the address they gave him.... Okay, I'll be here." He hung up. "There are more ways to choke a cat than by mental suggestion. I like the direct ways."

"You are most kind." I said humbly.

"Nuts!" he retorted. "People have helped me. Why shouldn't I help you?" His logic the way he saw it was unanswerable so I didn't try. We waited hardly ten minutes before the phone rang.

Danglos answered. "Yeah.... Metairie, eh, twenty-two-twenty-four Metairie Boulevard. That's fine, Jack. Do something for you some day ... bye."

Danglos wrote the address on an old envelope and handed it to me. Again hope surged through me and I felt like kissing him.

"Get the hell out of here!" he bellowed, palpably flustered by my incoherent thanks. "Come back and tell papa when you find that the landlord kicked her out and she left no forwarding address."

If I had been in any other frame of mind I dare say his jesting prognostication might have made an impression but it was not till a woman weighing some two hundred and fifty pounds came to answer my ring that I realized he might be a prophet after all.

"I am searching for a Miss Charles Kensington," I said.

"What a hell of a name for a Miss," roared the harridan, almost collapsing from mirth.

"I agree," I said holding on to my temper by main force, "that the name is somewhat odd. However ..."

"Odd, he says ... oh, my achin' back!" Again she screamed with mirth, slapping her adipose thigh.

"Is she here?" I asked sharply.

"No, honey, she isn't here," said the woman. "In fact, if she's the woman who was here before me, she's been gone some time."

"It is urgent that I get in touch with her," I explained. "Do you know whether she left a forwarding address?"

The large woman shook her head. "If she left it, honey, it ain't here now. I've had the place done over and I threw out everything...."

The only thing I could think of when the taxi driver asked for a destination was Slim Jim's.

Slim Jim welcomed me effusively as I took a seat. "What'll it be this time, Prof, another Collins?"

I eyed him severely for a moment then in a voice of hard inflexible command, I said, "Please remove the top from a pint bottle and set it before me ... bourbon. I will also require a container of water and two glasses."

Jim had seen too many people with that look I suppose, so he shook his head. "Can't hear you fer the wind howlin', Prof. If you wanta get drunk I'm right here to see that you get that way but not the way you got it figgered. If you wanta get conked out rapid-like I'll oblige with a bungstarter but you got it all wrong. Now, have you ever done any straight whiskey drinkin'?"

I admitted that I had not, adding that one must start some time.

"Good enough!" he said agreeably. "Let me pour you a small one...on the house, of course, then you try it and if you like it that way I'll serve 'em to you gradual like. If you get drunk like a gent, then I'll see that you get home safe and sound but you got the wrong slant...a pint at a time..." he shook his head lugubriously.

I began to feel a little foolish as his reasonable argument struck through so I let him serve me a small glass of bourbon. He put it on the bar along with a small glass of iced water. Emulating Danglos, I tossed the liquor down...that is, such was my intention but it did not go down, not all of it. Most of it sprayed directly back at Jim who, doubtless expecting some such occurrence, ducked neatly. If all the phials of hell had been poured down my gullet in one draught I'm certain the result could not have been worse. For five minutes I coughed, strangled, sputtered, and endured the guffaws of numerous patrons who, upon hearing my first brave words, had stopped their drinking to watch me.

After regaining a portion of my breath I wiped the tears from my eyes and sighed. In a strangled voice I said, "You were right, Jim...make it a Collins."

So I sat there and became sodden with Collins and when Danglos came in I could see him only as a blur. He walked over and eyed me disapprovingly. "Pickled...so she was gone?"

"She was gone," I blurted, and turning around, I buried my face in my arms and wept.

Danglos waited till the storm had passed then took me to a booth, feeling, I suppose, that I was making a spectacle of myself.

"Now tell me," he said.

So I told him what there was to tell. "She's gone and no for-warding address."

"Look … weepy. All is not lost even though you may feel it is. I can find the gal if you want me to—I'm just wondering whether I should."

I straightened up suddenly. "If you can find her and don't then you will favor me by never speaking to me again … you unspeakable cad."

He grinned "Hold it—I haven't said I wouldn't, but suppose I do. What then?"

It was not a question for a man awash with Collins to answer. In fact, had I been sober it would have made me think for a while. "Why, if you find her …"

"Yeah, I find her and if she's got a husband or something, what then?"

"Then I do not care what happens. Left alone … life will have lost its savor and the grave will beckon."

"Oh, cripes," he groaned. "Oh death where is thy sting, oh, grave where is thy victory?"

"Danglos," I said furiously, "you're making fun of me and I resent it."

"Then sit up like a man and go home before you get so stinko that it will take you a week to pull out. Come to see me tomor-row and we'll find the gal. Your blood being on your own head if it makes things worse, which I very much fear it will. Why did she run out? Why didn't she leave a forwarding address? Why a million things?"

He left me and after another Collins I decided to take his advice to go home. As I got into the taxi a thought struck me that left me staggered and I barked an address at the driver that was not my own. "And if on the way you see a likely place where one might purchase a Collins, I would deem it a great favor if you would dismount from this steed, purchase same and bring it back with you. Buy yourself a drink at the same time if you so desire."

The driver, whom I suppose had heard every manner of peculiar request, did not seem to think this at all unusual and before we reached my destination I had encompassed two more Collins and it was with two empty glasses in my hands that I knocked on the door of Miss Cannon's apartment and stood teetering to-and-fro, listening to the clop of the heels of her mules on the floor as she came to answer the knock.

"Miss Cannon," I said, striving for dignity, "I have come to ask you to be my wife and to share bed and fireside with me till death do us sunder ... er, I mean, tears us apart."

"Jesu Christu and General Jackson!" she ejaculated, stepping back a pace, "are you stuccoed?"

"I beg your pardon?"

"Come in before some creature of the night spots you before my door and sets tongues to wagging."

I entered the apartment, having considerable difficulty synchronizing the progress of my body and feet, one having a tendency to outstrip the other, which must have affected the grace of my carriage somewhat. I sat on the couch with a thump and eyed the glasses. "I started out with these glasses filled with Collins. In some manner unknown to me they have evaporated."

"Since they aren't spilled down your front then I can only suggest that you opened your mouth before you spilled them."

I nodded gravely. "The latter possibility appeals to me as the more logical of the—twick—pardon me, two. To get along with the proposition that I made an hour or so ago ...."

"It was only two minutes," she corrected caustically.

"Really ... how forgetful of me ... well tempus fick ... er, fugits, as the saying goes."

"Yes, and at the rate it's fugiting right now we'll have a spawn of brats before you leave."

"Miss Cannon, your remark smacks of the…shall we say, indelicate?"

"Call it downright nasty if it suits you. Say, what's gotten into you…? I mean, aside from the fact that you're steaming drunk."

"Merely condensation, Miss Cannon. The term steam suggests pressure and heat and I assure you…."

"Never mind the lecture on thermodynamics—you mentioned marriage."

"Yes, I feel that I should make an honest woman of you."

"What about you?"

"I am willing to accept my responsibility."

"Will it make an honest man of you?"

I considered this at some length for I had never heard it so neatly turned about and the novelty of it intrigued me. "I shall have to give the subject mature cogitation. It has an intriguing sound."

"Don't strain yourself, Mac. If you've got any mature cogitation, which I have been led to doubt, then you'd better hoard it."

"Will you marry me, Miss Cannon?" My tone was hard and inflexible or so I thought until I heard hers.

"No!" and a more uncompromising negative never smote my ears.

"May I ask why?"

"You may."

"Very well then—why?"

"Because you're immature, you're still in need of a keeper and I'm not it. Because when I marry I want strong support so that I may be as silly and irresponsible and giddy as I please and still know that this strong support is always with me."

"Miss Cannon," I said after I had been sobered somewhat by her blunt rejection, "I would like a Collins."

"You'll not get it here. I'll make you some strong coffee and if you're smart you'll go hold your head under that shower for a while."

I did so and emerged considerably refreshed and after two cups of strong coffee I felt relatively sober. It took some time for these operations and when at last she sat with me in the living room, her cigarette sending off blue curls of smoke, I felt quite ashamed of myself.

"I do beg your pardon, Miss Cannon, for this untimely visit and my idiotic maunderings."

"Then you didn't mean what you said about getting married?"

"Oh, yes, I meant that and I'm hoping you'll reconsider."

"Prof, I have mentioned before that I think you're a pretty swell guy, underneath I don't know what all, but I'm not the one to wrestle you out from your wrappings."

"I would bend my best efforts toward being a good husband, I assure you."

"You're in love with Charles. Right now you're sore at heart and miserable. You're grasping at a straw and I don't want to be it. I like you and I've enjoyed my part in pulling you out of yourself, but for keeps ... no. No husband is good because he breaks his back at the job. It's something that's in him or isn't. It wouldn't be much fun if you had to work at it. Any time you want to talk, get a little tight and brag about yourself, orate on the beauties of high thought, or any of your lovely little pastimes, I'll be glad to see you and you're welcome here any time I'm not otherwise occupied. But marriage for us wouldn't work."

"You're a wonderful person, Miss Cannon." I'm afraid my eyes were a little moist and I know that her avowal of friendship created a tightness in my throat. She came over to me and held my head against her breast which would have been no end comfortable had it not been so upsetting. I pulled her down and kissed her long and with every bit of my newly acquired finesse.

"Prof," she murmured hoarsely, "whatever else has been against you, you have developed into a boudoir buccaneer of no mean talent!"

I tried to be as quiet as possible that night but with her watch-dog sense of knowing when I'm about, Josy let me in again and again accompanied me to my bedroom where, due to my drink-ing, I suppose, was performed a marathon that left Josy in a state of bewildered and satiated delight and me in a state approaching death from which I did not wake till twelve the next day.

That lovely Josy. I wondered if she were not the girl I should marry!

CHAPTER EIGHT
HELP WANTED, MALE

"I HAVE BEEN," opened Danglos as I walked in that afternoon, "working on your case. It was a cinch and the details are all here."

I felt as though about to be attacked by a chill and I didn't at the moment press him for details because I was afraid.

"So we'll start by me telling you a story. Once upon a time there was a beautiful girl named Lenthe, pronounced Lentha. Lenthe lived with a crab of an old father who was too sick to live and too mean to die. He tottered around for years, a sort of ambulatory corpse, until one night in his sleep he was caught off guard and the Grim Reaper let him have it right smack in the ticker. Very neat death, all things considered. No gore, no expensive sheets tom, no *rus sardonicus* to indicate poisoning and nothing else of a dramatic nature. Just a quiet natural death. Well, it appears that Lucien Kensington died possessed of enough lucre to pay off the national debt, and as is the case with these birds, his will had enough clauses to make the lawyer earn his fifteen percent. One of the clauses was that Lenthe was to receive a handsome income till the age of twenty-one at which time she would be free to marry, and if she didn't marry she still got her income but not a cent of that vast stack of unsanitary lettuce. She was allowed her twenty-first year in which to make her decision, picking the man and stuff like that there. Now, Lenthe was a sane smart cookie and wouldn't have been worth a tinker's damn to anyone who wanted to write a book about a poor little rich gal who, weary of all that cash, said to hell with it, married the gardener for love and raised a ton of snotty brats. Not our Lenthe! She ups and snags the first pair of pants that seems to be inhabited by live flesh and bone and marries him, at the right time, and under the right sort of circumstances, to assure no questions asked when she wanted a million or so as pocket change. The picture you saw was a press release and kind of old. She's been married six months, has nothing to do with the usual pack of camp followers, spurns recently interested relatives and in general conducts herself as a fine lady with a mind of her own which, so far, few have been able to fathom. Her one stroke of bad luck was her choice of occupied pants who was smart enough to be handy and knew enough about people to figure that some such scheme might just possibly pop up. It popped and Denville Chatsworth Palmar, whom I have only just learned is plain Joe Gruber in a little town called Diddle, was there to catch the goose and now he is laying plans to make her bring forth some golden eggs. This, of course, all happened after the honeymoon which my Miami man says was spent in separate rooms. I doubt that Joe liked this but with such a reward hanging just within reach who's gonna quibble?"

"But she *is* married?" I put in.

"Yep. Married a cheap grifter who happened to be handy— but unluckily for her, pretty shrewd and determined to hang on to his wedding right."

I became excited. "If he married her under that long name then he married under false pretenses."

"He even thought of that and admitted to her that it wasn't his real name. On the license she is Mrs. Joseph Gruber. What did she care about a name?"

"Have you found her?"

"Yep.... I've done that, too. She ran off and left the husband but he didn't have too much trouble finding her and must have showed up the day you ran out on her. They are both at the Roosevelt."

I felt sick and must have turned white because Danglos laughed. "Hold it, pal, they're still registered separately."

I sat for a while trying to think what I should do, then I asked Danglos.

"You got me there," he said. "It could be that you might complicate things for her by showing up just now because if he could get something on her then he could make it tough for her to get a divorce. On the other hand one never knows. I've got the dope for you and from here on the ball's yours."

I sighed and sat back in the chair, so numb with misery that I couldn't think. Then it popped into my mind that Aunt Cam had wanted me to move into the French Quarter and now that Charles—Lenthe—was found, the thought of sleeping away out on State Street appalled me.

"I desire to secure living quarters in the French Quarter," I told Danglos and explained why I wanted them.

"Don't blame you. You might call my landlord .... Hold on, I'll call him for you."

Danglos dialed a number and after a few minutes of conversation he hung up.

"You're in luck. An apartment near mine, in an adjoining building, is being vacated tomorrow and if you'll slip him an extra ten under the counter he'll let you have it." So that afternoon I moved in, the operation not being such a task since I only had a few clothes and books to bring. As I rode toward Canal Street I looked back lazily over my life since that fateful night in September when Miss Cannon had performed her experiment. To say I had made strides would have been something short of the truth. So far the sex which had come my way was so ordered that I could hardly have avoided it save by dint of will and determination which I apparently did not possess. Of one thing I was certain, nothing that had ever happened to me before could match its ecstatic wonders. There had been three women and although they were as different from each other as the sun from the stars they each had delights of a different kind to offer. Of course in the case of Lenthe I was in love and that difference was the greatest.

I stifled a groan and closed my eyes, in which position I remained till we arrived at my new abode. As is the case of so many buildings in the French Quarter this was not in the least prepossessing from the outside but inside everything changed. There was a bedroom, bath, living room, quite a large one, dinette and a small kitchen. The furniture was old but rich in appearance and very comfortable. I stowed my clothes in a closet in the bedroom and puttered about putting this and that in place and had started to disrobe with the idea of taking a shower when I heard a veritable symphony go off in some hidden place. I assumed that it must be a kind of doorbell but I had never before heard one with so many notes.

I went to the door and admitted a girl appearing not a day over twenty—I subsequently learned that she was twenty-six—dressed in a simple print dress that was not remarkable in any manner save the fit which was breathtaking. Her hair was black and straight but so soft that it appeared, as had Lenthe's, to float, each strand separate from the others. She smiled, twin dimples deepening in her cheeks. "I'm Adrienne Danglos—and you're Professor Tallant?"

Something about this wistfully beautiful girl tugged at my heart. I smiled my best for her and said, "Please, let us not stand on formality. I consider your husband one of my very best friends and to them I am Tommy, Mac, and several less appropriate names." She offered her hand and I took it, noticing that her clasp was strong and hearty.

"I came to ask if you'd have dinner with us. We have a cook who can prepare the most divine food and we'd love to have you."

"And I will esteem it a great pleasure to dine with you," I replied.

At six forty-five, Danglos called me on the phone and told me to come on over as he was having a drink before dinner and there was no etiquette observed around his house anyhow. I dressed quickly and walked the few steps to his apartment to be admitted by a colored boy. "Come in, suh," he said with an exaggerated bow. "You're now in the house what somebody else built but what I cooks in and you ain't never et till you been fed by Efferson Jefferson, the One Two Three."

He ushered me into the living room while delivering this greeting, leaving me somewhat taken aback.

"That's his standard line," said Danglos, handing me a Collins which had the addition of some spice I could not identify.

"Where'n hell are the towels?" came a voice from deep within the bowels of the house, with a force sufficient to make the windows rattle.

"Stop screaming!" came a smaller voice that carried a great deal of authority and the roar subsided to a mutter over which could be heard Adrienne's melodious laughter.

"Company?" I asked.

He nodded. "From Baton Rouge…friends of mine. The man is practically a brother of the man who married Sundown Smith, now Roland. They have a new baby and couldn't come but Toussaint and his wife came to the Tulane-Tech game and stayed over." Until he mentioned the game I hadn't realized it was Sunday. Toussaint turned out to be a giant of a man, and must have weighed in the neighborhood of two hundred twenty pounds. His limbs were thick and brutally muscular yet they retained a remarkable degree of symmetry for all their size. His slim willowy wife, who had silenced him, was a quietly beautiful little thing, with eyes that twinkled humorously except when they regarded her husband; then they were wells of adoration.

Danglos stood as they came in. "Toussaint, meet Professor Tallant."

My hand seemed lost in the man's great paw and I refrained from crying out only with the greatest effort although I have been known to make grown men wince from the power of my grip. To him it was nothing and I was glad to be released.

Toussaint was an extrovert of some dimensions and it did not take long to place him. He loved fun, laughter, good food and, unless I was mistaken, good liquor. Danglos handed him a highball that lasted one gulp then had to be refreshed. Toussaint, as I discovered, had his serious side too and while conversation swirled about us he said quietly, "Dang is a particular friend of mine, Tallant, and I don't think you could call it a breach of confidence if he told me about you and he has. He told me because he knows that my partner and I … er … sort of take to adventure of various sorts and he thought that this problem might possibly produce work for us."

I was mystified and must have showed it. "You are very kind … but what sort of work?"

"There's a man in your way, isn't there?"

"Yes, but he has legal standing. I have none."

Toussaint grinned showing a large mouth, his sharp white teeth gleaming. "We don't work legally; we work in the dark. Now, of course, we'd never help him against you but since you're the underdog we're on your side. I have Dang's word for it that the man is a no-good, a cheat, a preyer on women—and we might be able to give you a hand if you want it."

I shook my head. "What you suggest, Mr. Toussaint, is quite out of the question. The man is Lenthe's legal husband and I'm afraid there isn't anything to be done about it."

We didn't get a chance to discuss the matter further because the conversation included us about that time and we were drawn into as delightful a bit of chitchat as I have ever experienced. They were a very appreciative audience and after several Collins

I managed to inject a few rather racy anecdotes which reaped gales of laughter, a most welcome change from the way they are usually received.

The dinner came up to every expectation and the more we ate the more Jefferson beamed.

We assured him that his cooking was indeed superlative. After dinner I made my excuses as soon as was fitting and left, having things other than light conversation on my mind. Hailing a passing cab, I gave an address only a block from the Roosevelt Hotel. As my apartment is on Royal Street it was only a short run to Canal where I got out of the cab, paid the driver and walked across the wide throughfare and down Baronne Street to the entrance of the hotel.

For an hour I wandered aimlessly about in the richly appointed lobby watching for Lenthe but no sign of her did I see. I bought a package of cigarettes of a mild brand and sat smoking them, feeling that I must do something but sensitive to the knowledge that I must seem a tyro to anyone who was not. An ill-timed inhalation drew a quantity of smoke into my lungs reacting almost as vigorously as had the drink of straight whiskey at Slim Jim's and when I finally recovered my breath and wiped the tears from my eyes I saw the retreating form of Lenthe headed for the elevators. I leaped to my feet and made a dash in her direction, calling on her to stop. She kept going and halted before the closed doors of an elevator landing.

"Charles," I gasped catching her by the arm. She turned and looked at me with the eyes of a stranger.

"I beg your pardon." Her voice was edged and chilly. I fell back a pace or two with astonishment knowing very well that I was not mistaken.

A hand fell upon my arm. "Beat it, pal...."

It was the rat-faced gentleman I had seen in the picture with her.

"You will unhand me this instant," I said furiously, "or I shall be forced to break your limbs."

He laughed nastily. His face was sneering and what with Lenthe's cold reception I quite lost my temper. Pivoting slightly to gather momentum, I brought the sharp edge of my right hand down on his right wrist where it was holding my left sleeve. My fury lent considerable power to the blow and I had the satisfaction of hearing the wristbone snap like a stick of hard candy. The rat-faced man screamed and fell back against the wall whereupon I attacked him with a ferocity hitherto unknown to me. I smacked a solid left under his jaw and buried my right in his stomach as hard as I could and when he fell to the floor I pounced upon him and was beating him with both fists, sobbing with rage and chagrin, when several hands attempted to drag me from him. I whipped backward with an elbow at the man to my right, catching him in a most vulnerable and tender spot and the clutching hands became unfriendly. I leaped to my feet, ramming a knee into the groin closest to me with telling effect, and rendering another *hors de combat* with a precise chop to the neck before a sudden blackness descended over me.

Some time later I woke up dizzy with a lump the size of an egg adorning my cranium, and a sense of total disorientation. I seemed to be in a cage of sorts with bars all about me and I lay on a cot that was not overly clean and decidedly uncomfortable. I sat up, holding my head in my hands, till the vertigo subsided some-what, then I examined my cage carefully. As I had suspected, there didn't seem any means of easy egress except a door which was locked, and as I had no key I was balked. There seemed to be a long line of similar cages in which reposed other citizens all of whom seemed to be in even worse shape than I. One sat on his cot reciting tedious poetry without end, disregarding entirely all manner of abuse which was being cast at him from other inmates upon whose nerves the recitation grated.

"Why," I asked a man in the cage next to mine, "am I here?"

"That's a good question, mate," said the wizened little fellow. "They all ask it, but it's still a good question."

Nevertheless he made no attempt to answer so I sat again on the hard cot and considered my lot. Obviously my being here was in some manner connected with my late fracas in the lobby of the hotel; then it struck me. My blood seemed to congeal in my veins and an icy perspiration dampened my brow. Looking about the place again, I was now certain that I was in jail.

"It would appear," I said to the little man, "that I have been incarcerated."

"So it would," he said puckishly but I was not in the mood for badinage.

"Who is the proprietor of the establishment?" I asked.

"I have never met the gentleman formally," piped the little man who used surprisingly good English and for all his dilapidated looks, too. "However, you might ... soon."

If I seem a little ill informed as regards jails I must point out that I had never been in one before. A man dressed in a blue uniform whom I took to be a policeman came and unlocked my door.

"Okay, chum—you can come out now."

I walked from the cell and down a corridor which let out into a large room with a raised desk at which sat another man in a blue uniform.

"Well, the human buzz saw is come to life!" he said derisively.

"I wish to know why I have been incarcerated," I said walking straight up to the desk and looking the man in the eye.

"Because, me boy," said the man, "we can't have people beating up citizens in the lobby of the town's plushiest hotel and trying to kill half a dozen others who tried to stop it."

"He richly deserved a much worse beating than I gave him," I said defensively.

The man chuckled deep in his chest. "Doubtless he did, but I might point out that if you had done a better job you might be here on a charge of murder. It so happened that upon looking through your effects I noticed an address which had been written on an envelope addressed to my good friend Mr. Danglos, and he is bailing you out."

He waved a hand and I looked toward the other side of the room. There stood Danglos, Toussaint, both their wives, and a swarthy gentleman with a heavy moustache whom I did not know. I flushed heavily, feeling that I had been caught in a very uncomfortable position and had also caused some trouble. They came over to me, laughing at my embarrassment, but in spite of that I was glad to see them. They introduced me to a Lieutenant Pizzo who was not wearing a uniform but nevertheless was a policeman.

"Not many things left for you to do," said Danglos, clapping me companionably on the shoulder, "now that you've got jail under your belt. How do you feel?"

"I feel fit except for a headache," I replied.

"One of my men had to whack him a love tap to subdue him," said the man behind the desk. "He was very belligerent."

"He can be at times," said Danglos. "Will there be anything more?"

Pizzo at this juncture took charge. "Not unless the assaulted man prefers charges. He might be satisfied if you paid his hospital bill, Mr. Tallant."

I left them, feeling a warm glow of friendship for these wonderful people, the conviction again being visited upon me that I had been indeed blind to think that association with persons who were not intellectual giants was a waste of time. I sat in my living room and gave myself over to misery, for some time wondering upon the fact that Lenthe had turned a cold shoulder to me, the only ray of hope being that maybe she did not want Palmar to know that she was acquainted with me. Since he was now in the hospital, there was no reason I shouldn't talk to her so I called the hotel and asked for her room.

She answered the phone and my heart gave a leap. "It is Thomas, Charles...."

"I'm sorry," her voice was cold and formal, "you must have the wrong room."

She hung up. I cradled the receiver and sank back into a chair where I sat for some time in numb misery.

A noise in my bedroom made me turn around. "I've got it all cleaned up now, sir. The beds made and turned down. I've vacuumed the place and it's real clean now." It was a girl, about Josy's shade of rich coffee. "Who are you?" I managed to get out.

She smiled, and like Josy she had beautiful teeth. "I'm Valentine Valtin, sir. I'm Josy's cousin. She said she'd like to come clean up for you but she lives at Miss Cam's and it's so far."

She was well knit but where Josy was overblown and and superbly fleshy this girl was as slim and graceful as a dancer. Her movements were feral and beautifully coordinated. Her face was inclined to narrowness, pointed, and her mouth was small but full-lipped, somewhat more carefully chiseled than Josy's. The eyes were almond-shaped and definitely slanted, which heightened the catlike cast of her face. One could not say whether she was Josy's superior as regards looks because they were of such different types.

My gaze must have been too intent because she colored a little and said, "I'll put your shirts and underwear away, then I'll go. Unless you'd like me to make you a drink."

"I have no materials for drinks," I told her.

"Oh, I went to the liquor store and bought some things."

"Uh... you did? Where did you get the money?"

"You left twenty dollars on the dresser. I put the change back."

"I... er, yes, of course. That was very thoughtful of you. Can you make a Tom Collins?"

"The best you ever tasted."

"Excellent! You may make me one before you leave."

"Yes, sir." She went back into the bedroom where she puttered about for fifteen minutes then she made a Collins for me and brought it out. It was, as she had said, the best I had ever tasted.

I looked at her keenly. "You speak very well, Valentine. I take it that you've been to school."

"Yes, sir. High-school graduate and a certificate from Business College."

"And you make your living as a house girl?"

"Yes, sir. For every stenographic job in this town there must be ten candidates and to be truthful, sir, I wouldn't say I'm the best graduate they ever turned out."

"Well, I must say you take it philosophically. Many would be resentful."

"Resentful people are unhappy people, sir. Resentment is not, as you probably know, necessarily the result of an injustice. There are people of whom resentment is as much a part as the lack of it is a part of me."

"You evidence extraordinary perception, Valentine, which I doubt that you picked up in business college."

She smiled and her entire face lit up. "I read, I think, and I apply what reason I can to my life."

This vivid colored girl rather amazed me. Her lucidity, solid philosophy and keen penetration were astounding.

"Then you are happy…the way life is situated for you? Wouldn't you prefer living in the north where your opportunities might be greater?"

"I'm happy here," she said simply and seriously, "whereas if I went up there I might not be. Ambition can be a disease and in my present state I only want to be free to pursue my natural inclinations. Happiness as I see it is not a state of being but a state of becoming. It, like so many emotions, depends on imponderables in many cases. There are people who have what we would say is every reason to be happy and are not, while many with no apparent reason are. As a state for living I'll take comfort and contentment plus whatever sprays of happiness I can decorate them with."

I handed her my glass. "Henceforward, Valentine, do not consider yourself a servant but a friend."

Her smile was soft and I thought I could even detect a touch of affection in it. "Thank you, sir. I consider that a great compliment."

"Would you like to fix a drink for yourself?"

"No, sir. I'll drink with you some time but I have a date tonight as soon as I'm through."

I frowned. "Go on to your date. Whatever you have to do can be done in easy stages. There's no reason to do it all in one night."

Again her brilliant smile flashed. "Thank you. I'll fix you another Collins and leave." She came back in a few moments with the drink and then left for her date. I sat sipping my drink and considering how thoroughly she had thought everything out for herself. She was of the type that could see a truth and face it. I felt that I was rapidly reaching the same state but I couldn't say that I had arrived. Lenthe came into my mind again in full force and I almost wept with rage and despair. I even thought of contacting Mr. Toussaint to see if he would consent to use some of his extralegal methods to persuade Palmar or Gruber to give her the divorce. But the conviction swept down upon me that even if she were free she might wish no part of me. Maybe that glorious night had been to her a mere surcease from boredom, something she now wished to forget.

I took a hot shower, topped off with a stinging cold one, and went to bed. I had envisioned rolling and tossing hours, but I had been through a lot that day and my tired body succumbed at once.

CHAPTER NINE
DINNER FOR TWO

T HE next morning I slipped into a robe and walked into the dinette where I could see that Valentine had come and was preparing breakfast.

"Good morning," she said brightly. "Have a seat and I'll pour you a starter."

A starter turned out to be a cup of coffee that tasted like no coffee I ever had drunk before.

"What is this?" I said, eyeing the cup with reverence.

"Coffee," she said, 'with a tot of spiced brandy."

"Delicious!" I said and tasted it again. The spiced brandy seemed to intensify the flavor of the bean, the result being a gastronomic delight and somewhat more stimulating than the plain. So it was with a generous appetite that I attacked the breakfast. This brought a gleam of joy to Valentine's brown eyes. I sat back and took a cigarette and watched her through the door as she flitted gracefully about in the kitchen, admiring her slim smooth legs and the willowy motion of her body. Having by now become breast-conscious I gave hers the required attention and noted that they were large but quite pointed, tenting the material of her dress delightfully. A wave of hot blood swept over me.

I wandered about that day, lonely, miserable, with the aimless gait of a somnambulist. I had told Valentine that I would not require lunch so there was nothing to go home for. In midafternoon I found myself on Bourbon Street so I walked the few intervening blocks to Slim Jim's.

He greeted me effusively, as usual, and in a matter of seconds had a Collins before me.

"Jim, do you recall the lady with whom I left your establishment the first night I came here?"

"Sure do, Prof. Say, wasn't she a looker? Saw her again yesterday."

I was staggered for a moment. "What … she was here?"

"Sure was. Sittin' right in the same booth as the night she and you met."

"At what time?" I asked excitedly.

"Oh—about this time, I'd say. She sat there for a while and nibbled on one drink and then got up and left."

"Did she converse with anyone while she was here?"

"Nope. I watched her, cause I remembered you had took a shine to her. She just gave her order to the waiter and that was all there was to it."

I slumped on my stool and said no more. A chance visit, no more, no less—in the middle of the afternoon.

At six or thereabouts the phone behind the bar rang and Jim answered it. He glanced at me and put the instrument on the bar. "For you, Prof."

I picked up the receiver and said, "Hello."

"Mr. Tallant, this is Valentine. Dinner will be ready in half an hour."

"But," I protested, "I don't want any dinner."

"We have fresh king mackerel broiled in lemon butter sauce with a faint touch of garlic, tossed salad, broccoli, hot pocketbook rolls, and plum jam. There's a banana cream pie for dessert."

"But Valentine, you shouldn't …."

"It's a little chilly so I made a fire in the living room. It's real pretty and the place is sort of half-dark and comfy."

"Very well, Valentine. I'll be home in a few minutes. But tell me, how did you know I was here?"

"I called Josy. She told me to call Mr. Danglos. He told me that at a guess, the most likely place to find you would be at Slim Jim's."

"Your solicitude is touching," I told her.

I left Jim's with the feeling that a longer wait was fruitless, that Lenthe wouldn't show up and even if she did she would not want to see me. When I arrived at the apartment I hardly knew the place. A cheery fire blazed in the tiny grate and in place of electric lights Valentine had placed candles which threw a soft voluptuous light over the stately old furniture and the cream-colored walls. She came into the living room with a Collins for me and I was struck by her appearance. She wore a very simple dress of dull red wool which was cut very low at the neck exposing a considerable area of milky tan skin that had the sheen of old ivory. Her hair was severely parted in the middle and done into two buns which nestled at the nape of her neck, giving her oriental face an accentuation that was bafffingly attractive.

"Thanks," I said. "I've been drinking at Jim's but I'm afraid he was serving me little else than lemonade. I was distraut and didn't notice."

She eyed me sympathetically for a moment. "Mr. Tallant, you're unhappy, aren't you?"

I shrugged. "Yes, I am. Since September I have striven might and main to become a person of passable intelligence and have tried to fit myself into the scheme of social existence. But I suffered a blow that has made me unhappy. However, don't worry about it. I shall, no doubt, in time recover and I do appreciate your concern."

Her smile was like a shot in the arm. "If you can admit that then you're all right inside, sir. It will take time for you to catch up but you'll make it. Dinner will be on the table in ten minutes."

I sat pondering and drinking, hypnotizing myself in the flickering flames of the fire, until at length she called me to dinner. I went in and sat at the small table set with spotless linen and sparkling crystal and silver.

"I seem to have seen this silver before," I mused aloud, fingering a salad fork.

"Yes, sir," she put a luscious brown fillet of mackerel before me. "Miss Cam sent it over. The place didn't have any silver or china fit for a dog so I called her and she sent it over."

I had to chuckle. "The way women order my life! I come in last night and find you have taken over. Now Aunt Cam sends china and silver and you drag me bodily from a comfortable seat at a bar to a dinner I didn't want. Now I'm enjoying it and feel hungry as a bear."

She placed her finely sculptured hands on the back of a chair. "Are you sorry I came, sir?"

I grinned at her, my mouth full of succulent fish. "Don't be silly. I'm tickled to death."

She went back into the kitchen and brought more food, opening a steaming metal dish filled with soft fragrant rolls, then she went back and sat in the kitchen. I glanced across the table and looked at the empty space and gradually my mastication slowed and came to a stop. For a long moment I stared at the spot then I spoke. "Valentine?"

She leaped up with smooth grace and came into the dinette. "Yes, sir?"

I pointed with my knife, a vulgar habit which I do not have really, but it seemed necessary to be as imperious as I could. "Please set another plate." She gave me a blank look but did as I asked in her usual swift, efficient manner. "Now will you take off that apron?" She did so, slowly, her eyes questioning but steady. "Now sit down and have dinner with me … I shall consider it a favor, if you will."

She stood very still for a moment.

I feigned anger. "Sit down here and have dinner with me. There's more than enough food, there's room, and I despise eating alone. Now sit down and eat."

A slow smile started across her face that grew brighter and wider until at last a little gurgle of a laugh sounded. "Mr. Tallant, you know … somehow I just wanted you to ask me to eat with you."

I felt absurdly pleased and I believe I flushed a little. "Thank you, Valentine."

We ate at a decorous pace, enjoying our food and hurrying not at all. The girl's table etiquette was flawless, considerably better than my own in fact and I grinned inwardly at the thought that should some of my acquaintances see me now they'd be surprised, possibly shocked. I, on the other hand, was enjoying myself greatly as was Valentine and I'd wager her reasons while not similar sprang from the same seed. I watched her as she ate, her face composed and delectable in the candlelight, a face that by any standards was really beautiful. Her hair, burnished jet in color, reflected the reddish glow of the candle flame like polished metal. Suddenly I had an impulse and succumbed to it.

"Will you do me a favor, Valentine?"

"Why—certainly, sir."

"Will you take your hair down?"

The brightest light in the room was her smile because she knew exactly why I had asked, knew that I admired her hair and would relish the sight of it in the soft light. Without a word she withdrew two pins and shook her head, making the tresses fall in rich thick layers about her shoulders. She put her hands under them and shook them out so that they glistened with reflected light. Valentine's hair shimmering like lacquered satin in the candlelight! My throat constricted and I felt a dampness of the eye.

I didn't say anything. I just looked and the look was probably better applause than I could have delivered by word of mouth for she reached out and squeezed my hand gently.

"Thank you so much, Mr. Tallant."

"What?...Oh." I felt embarrassed for I realized when she spoke that I had been staring at her with a sort of hypnotized fixity. When I realized what had made her say it I was instantly struck with the fact that again she had shown something approaching second-sight. She knew exactly what was going on in my mind.

We finished the dinner in silence and I rose and went into the living room to relax. I could head her clearing the table, washing dishes, and stowing them away in the china closet. It was a comfortable sound and I realized that Valentine was no less than a godsend. I could think of Lenthe with less pain because I knew I had a close, understanding friend.

Some forty-five minutes later she came into the living room. "Have a date tonight, Valentine?" I asked.

"No, sir. Not tonight."

'What are you going to do?"

"Nothing, sir. I'm through now and..."

"Yes?"

"Well, I guess I'll go home unless you wouldn't mind me sitting and talking to you."

"The idea!" I scoffed. "You know, I'd be delighted to have you talk to me. Take off your apron and let's talk."

She hesitated a moment. "Please, sir ... may I use the bathroom for a moment? I want to comb my hair and touch up my face."

"Of course, you may use it at any time you choose."

There was a bear rug in front of my fireplace and Valentine had vacuumed it assiduously the day before and now it was quite clean. I stretched out on it before the fire as I used to do when I was a child. The hardwood burned steadily, giving off a cheery light, making joyful little noises as fires do, making me feel very peaceful in spite of my misery. Remembering the play of flickering flame on the walls from times past I got up and extinguished the candles. I returned to the rug and stretched out again, looking fixedly into the flames.

Valentine came out of the bathroom, her hair sending off sparks from the illumination of the fire, waving about her shoulders in soft masses. "Sit here on the rug," I said. "I feel like I was about twelve, through with my lessons and all prepared for a stint of dreaming."

She sat with a single fluid motion and turned on one hip, drawing her feet up behind, supporting her upper body with her left hand. "Firelight seems to have a sort of hypnotic action upon me," she said.

"I've noticed a similar effect. There's nothing quite like an open fireplace as an aid to dreams. What do you dream of, Valentine, at times like this?"

She thought for a while, her face catching the ruddy emanations from the fire, making each feature oddly beautiful. Some of her hair slid forward over her shoulders to caress her cheeks and my heart pumped faster at the sight. "I dream of a home of my own and, of course, children. I dream of pretty clothes and…" she smiled apologetically, "pretty filmy expensive underthings, and—men."

"Do you dream much of men?"

"More than I should, I suppose; but so few of them really attract me. For every date I have that is really enjoyable there are ten that are not."

"Are you in love?"

"Not enough to marry anybody. I'm a very affectionate person and I won't deny that I like to love…to play at it, rather, because it stimulates me and I am human. One must have affection and caresses. They're important to emotional welfare."

How well I knew the truth of that. "For someone who has been starved as long as I, it is more than just important, it is vital."

Her soft eyes turned on me and for a moment she watched me with gentle compassion. "I knew that, sir, as soon as I saw you, or at least after I had talked to you."

I grinned wryly. "You mean it sticks out like that?"

"It is noticeable enough. Shall I fix you a drink?"

"Yes, and fix yourself one at the same time. Make mine good and strong because I feel logy."

She departed and in a little while came back with a bottle of gin, limes, a long spoon, a thermidor of ice, and glasses. She mixed the drinks.

The warmth of the fire, the sting of the drink on my stomach, the exotic beauty of the girl who sat beside me, all worked together to produce a restlessness in my blood and a growing desire that somehow she would pave the way toward greater things.

"Have you thought what a novelty it is to me, sitting here like this conversing with you, in your house under these cozy conditions, drinking with you with all the advantages of an equal?"

I nodded. "I think the novelty was one of the motivating factors of my invitation. I wanted to see how you would react. You carried it off like it was something you had been doing all your life."

She smiled. "And yet it is my first time. I had a white friend once whom I suppose was in love with me but he could never forget that I was colored. There was always the condescension, the attitude that I should please him above every other consideration, without any thought of me. When I stopped seeing him it made him wild with misery and I had a lot of trouble with him, yet not once would he admit that he loved me. Why is it, Mr. Tallant, that white men find colored women so attractive but so rarely admit affection for them?"

I sighed. "It is a psychological matter that springs from the old slave-master relationship and what they like to call white supremacy. Things of that nature, Valentine, die very hard. I cannot be called typical because I was not reared in the South and even had I been I dare say the full effect of it would not have reached me just as so many other things never reached me. I do not feel self-conscious in admitting that I have a great affection for Josy because she likes me, she misses no opportunity to do me a favor, and she waits on Aunt Cam hand and foot. I am certain that Aunt Cam feels a tremendous affection for Josy and your mother nor would she deny it."

"Josy certainly likes you, sir, I know that. She had told me so much about you that I found myself liking you before I ever saw you."

I wondered, my face growing uncomfortably warm, just how much Josy had told her.

"That there should be affection between you and me," I continued, "was inevitable because we understand each other so well."

I sat up and regarded her steadily. "I can even conceive of loving you, Valentine, but I say that merely in a conversational sense as I am already in love with another woman."

Her smile was thanks enough. "I'm glad you said it, sir, even as a possibility."

We had another drink and I noticed that Valentine's ivory cheek was somewhat flushed and her eyes brighter. After the third drink she lay back on the rug and stretched sinuously with the most delightful feline grace, and a gurgle of laughter escaped her throat.

"What's funny?" I wanted to know.

"Nothing. I was just thinking that I ought to be going home and here I lie in a very undignified position in the company of a white man, drinking his liquor and feeling just as much at home as if I were under my own roof. It isn't natural; but it's true."

I looked at the heavy black veil of her hair as it lay fanshaped on the white fur of the rug. "I'm glad you feel that way—it's the way I want you to feel."

With a single movement she rolled over, kissed the back of my hand and massaged her face against it. An electrifying sensation shot up the arm and my ears began to thud heavily. In rolling over her dress had come up, revealing several inches of golden thigh which did not act as a soporific. The old familiar symptoms were beginning to assert themselves and I heard myself as from a distance. "Why did you do that, Valentine?"

She looked up and smiled. "Because you are good and kind and your words make me go soft inside. I hope you don't mind."

"I didn't mind it at all, in fact, it was quite a sensation. One that might be improved upon."

She sat up and spun around so that her back was to the fire and her face toward me, her shoulder touching my knee. Her eyes were wide and soft, a kind of wondering light in them, and her lips were moist and smooth, parted lightly, the better to accommodate her increased respiration. For an unconscionable length of time we just looked at each other, wonder dawning simultaneously. Her lips moved with tiny twitches to the call of some emotion and words came forth in a whisper. "You really mean that?"

I nodded slowly and my voice was husky. "I really mean it."

And as those things will happen, we gradually closed the distance between us, her face coming up to meet mine, her eyes closing. Her lips were soft and tremulous against mine and her body was a willow wand in my arms as her hair poured over my arms and knees in a flood of the softest ebony.

When at last I released her she clutched me and buried her face in my chest holding me with hard pressure. I felt a sting of conscience and gently I lifted her face by cupping my hand under her chin. "Look at me, Valentine. I'm not being at all fair to you."

I was somewhat surprised to see her vixenish smile. She raised her face and kissed me gently. "Mr. Tallant, I like you an awful lot but I'm not in love with you. I expect nothing from you, beyond tonight. It's sweet of you to be concerned though and I'm delighted with you for it."

The embrace that followed seemed to prove her contention.

I came to a state approaching consciousness some time later and found her body resting on mine, my head veiled with her hair. I was keenly aware of the pressure of her sharp breasts on my chest. At my move, she raised her head and looked down at me, lowering her lips to mine in a long gentle kiss.

"You don't have to go home, do you?" I asked.

"No, sir. I don't have to."

Somewhat timidly, I placed my arm around her. Somewhat shyly, she raised her lips to be kissed.

I accepted the invitation, hotly placing my mouth upon hers, whereupon all timidity and shyness vanished. Suddenly the two of us had become bold as brass.

We indulged, thereafter, in all manner of shameless pursuits, including wild wrestling, dancing, even cuffing and spanking. These things served to rouse us both to fever pitch, and again and again I crossed the unutterably wonderful threshold of her womanhood. I shall never forget the long, slim legs of her—the golden body in the red firelight—the wondrous smoothness of her velvet skin—the ecstasy of her breasts. All mine to take, to enjoy, to conquer. Truly, this Valentine bestowed the bliss of the gods upon me, for in her way she was a goddess.

I woke at dawn the next morning and Valentine came in wheeling a little four-wheeled affair upon which reposed a delicious breakfast of smoothly scrambled eggs, piping hot biscuits, broiled ham and coffee.

"I hope you didn't mind me wearing your robe, sir. I'd like to bathe before I dress, if I may …"

I smiled. "The place is yours. Let me thank you again for a truly wonderful night." Her smile warmed me so that I almost forgot the pain in my heart. She sat and watched me eat, joining me in a cup of coffee at my insistence.

"I ate earlier while you were sleeping," she said. I drank two cups of coffee and topped the breakfast with a small glass of cold water, having something of a thirst. She wheeled the little vehicle from the room and came back through the living room to pick up her clothes where they had been tossed the night before. When she came back into the bedroom, I went to the desk where I made out a check for fifty dollars. "Here, take this and get all the underthings you want."

Her face became ecstatic when she looked at the check and she grinned like a child, "You're wonderful, Mr. Tallant."

I looked at her and shook my head. "If I am, Valentine, it is you that makes me that way."

But to my astonishment, she tore the check to shreds.

CHAPTER TEN
BENEFIT OF CLERGY

THREE o'clock found me walking distractedly along a street, the name of which I can't recall. I missed soothing effects of Valentine and my misery descended on me again to such an extent that I walked blindly as in a daze. When a gentleman suddenly took it upon himself to stop me, I was impelled to anger, but the gentle tone of his voice immediately calmed me.

"Many people have found it relieving to talk to me, my boy."

"Only the grave..." I began cutting the remark in half as I could picture Danglos' cynical eyes pronouncing me melodramatic.

"Scarcely an original conclusion," answered the cleric. I had now sufficiently stabilized myself to recognize his profession. "Many have tried it but it still remains to us here a debatable point whether such action is productive of its desired aim. Now, would you like to talk to me?"

I shrugged. "It could hardly make matters worse," I conceded.

He led me into the confines of an immense church which I shall not name for a reason you will readily understand. He did not lead me to the altar or pulpit or whatever it was called, but into a little anteroom furnished with a table and comfortable leather chairs. I sat down and shook my head to clear away the miasmic scattering of what might be called thoughts, save that none seemed to make the slightest sense.

The little man sat opposite me and clasped his hands in his lap.

"Do you wish to tell me what your problem is?" he asked.

I told him, feeling strangely comforted merely by relating it. I told him all, even my recently acquired taste for the flesh.

He nodded judicially and not in the least disapprovingly. "I rarely make mistakes about people—because I don't try judge them. Mine is not to judge, although some of my colleagues seem to think differently. However, I would like to know something of your background before I speak, thereby acquiring some knowledge of your requirements. I am not a man who quotes tracts as a cure-all for humanity as I know too much of humanity to make any such dreadful error."

I was mildly surprised at this attitude. Willingly, I gave him a brief sketch of my life, education, and recent confusion, making it plain why I suffered as I did.

For some time after I stopped speaking, he looked fixedly at nothing, his hands clasped. Then he spoke.

"I shall not need to tell you that much of your trouble is conflict arising from behavior patterns set up during your formative years. You know this."

"Yes. I know it, but there seems to be little advantage in the knowledge. It is not confusion as to what I should do that balks me, but the strength to do it. I should forget this woman and return to my post, where I should then proceed to be the man I never was previously. You speak of behavior patterns as a man who knows something of my profession."

"Plenty," said the little man. "Knowledge is not all to be found in one book. This is, of course, the rankest heresy, and to another I might not reveal what I'm telling you. However, you are a man with intelligence and education and I shall strive to insult neither. Now, I shall endeavor to point out some things which may shock, you coming from a man of the cloth. First, let me say that long ago I dedicated myself to aiding my fellow man. That is one vow which I hold sacred over any I may have made to God. I give God credit for being three or four degrees removed from an ass and therefore possessed of a sense of humor and a forgiveness greater than any theologian could ever admit if he wanted to continue in his field For a man of less intelligence than you, I would sympathize, pray, and hold forth mightily in abstruse and unintelligible terms on Higher Things and the wonders of the Immortal Soul. To you, I'll speak as one man to another. In this day, Mr. Tallant, we are taught in the church and in our schools what should be. You and I know that what is, need not be. For example, when you studied government in high school, you were taught that Congress was an able group whose passionate desire was only that of discharging their duties to the best of their ability. The president was a man of the most incorruptible majesty and nobility. Lesser politicians had so often and with such ponderous rhetoric assured us of their individual and collective excellence that we believed them. Let us now take a view of the facts. Congressmen have been convicted of bribery, connivance, trickery of the vilest sort. Presidents of United States have been known to possess, to exhibit something less than nobility, at times. But were you informed of any of these possibilities when you were in school or given any hint as to how to combat them?"

I shook my head.

"You were told," he continued, "what should be, but you were not told what is. Nothing is mentioned about corrupt police, politicians giving protection to gangsters when they had sworn to protect the people they represent. Not a word of this was taught you. You had to learn it in diverse ways and suffer the inevitable disillusionment. We are so fond of showing how the American Way is superior to all others that we become hypnotized into believing it is perfect when our intelligence should tell us nothing is perfect. In church, you are told what to do in order that you be presented upon death with a ticket to heaven. Even this has been commercialized and there are many who feel that they are buying their tickets when all they are buying is a little escape from the clamor of their consciences. Yet a conscience is little more than a conglomeration of behavior patterns set up by all the multifarious agencies to which we are exposed during our formative years. The only thing about it that can be said to be inherent is the individual capacity for it. Since individuals differ, capacities differ, and consciences differ. We might start with what is called a national conscience and work backward to what we could call an in-the-dark personal conscience. But each is different from the other due to varied personal manifestations. There never have been ten people who, of their own energy of mind, thought exactly alike without reservation on any given subject.

"Let us now come to the matter of personal desires and requirements. They too differ with the individual and to set up a dead level for human conduct is to distort every man to whom it is applied. Some it will distort by elevation, others by depression, and in neither state will you find the true man but a man, to some degree beset by conflict, altering both his mind and his body to whatever degree he is affected over and above his abilities of compensation. If I have five hundred Christians in my parish, then I have five hundred individuals who are Christians to whatever extent they are able. I do not have five hundred four-square, tried-and-true, twenty-two carat Christians. This same rule may be applied on to infinity. The only difference being that the further we go, the greater becomes the extreme with every conceivable degree of difference in between. We dare not say this openly, however. If we did, by far the majority of our people would be cast into gloom and have a problem to chew over which would strain their powers of mastication to the breaking point. Never, Mr. Tallant, require a dull person to think. It is the most demoralizing thing that can possibly happen to him. He will take it just far enough to become frightened and he does not have the ability to proceed into enlightenment. If, at a stretch of the imagination we said he did, then he'd probably blow out his brains because the light would be too bright."

The more the old gentleman spoke, the straighter I sat, till I was practically sitting on the edge of my chair.

"I find this probably the most remarkable discourse to which I have ever listened," I said breathlessly.

He smiled gently. "I can understand that. Did you ever read John Burroughs?"

"Yes, I have but I'm afraid I put him down hurriedly."

"John Burroughs once said there was a certain minimum in which the average man must believe in his own particular way, else he would feel that the universe had fallen out from under him. One can see the truth of this assertion on every hand. What, indeed, drives people to believing some of their utterly preposterous theorems unless it is the conviction that unless they have a fast opinion fixed in their mind, some cataclysm might result?

"Lord Halifax once remarked, I believe it was he, to a man of the cloth who apparently had taken him to task about some belief, that he believed what he could and felt certain that God would forgive him if he did not have the digestion of an ostrich. You would be surprised, nevertheless, how many people whose own digestion, if it actually came to that, would not equal that of a sparrow. Yet they will gulp belief meekly, by a dint of the most astounding vacuity that it is possible to imagine … because, if they didn't, the universe might fall from under them. Burroughs pointed out that it was man's supreme, almost unbelievable vanity that brought about this feeling. The conviction that the universe and all its wonders were created for man alone. He pointed out further that man, when in this frame of mind, thought only of the good and forgot that he was wearing shoes to keep out thorns, glass, and snake bites—clothes to keep out the cold, avoid poison ivy. He concluded further that if man thought of the matter at all and finally admitted that there were some things inimical to his well-being he immediately plastered the blame on the devil, a handy individual if there ever was one ... almost as handy as an anthropomorphic conception of God."

"I take it that you don't go along with the idea," I said.

The little man smiled and sat back. "I serve my fellow creature and if I can do so by handing out what he wants in the matter of spiritual unguent, then I do so. What I believe myself is another and unrelated matter entirely. The clergy, Mr. Tallant, is full of good, solidly intelligent men and if, at times, they appear to flounder in their own fat, so to speak, remember that in matters of public utterance they either hew to the mark or they are thrown ignominiously from the flock amid jeers and the casting of stones, the flock forgetting what was said by Jesus regarding same."

I drew in a deep breath. "Since September, I have been progressing along a road full of despair and fraught, as you pointed out, with disillusionment. But I think I am making progress. Beneath the layers of behavior patterns there is a lusty spirit which will, in the final accounting, emerge victorious."

He nodded. "Man strives to force himself into patterns because they are offered him at an unprotesting age by people whom he has learned either to respect or fear. He accepts the order and performs to whatever extent this primitive underlying spirit which we will call the *id* will allow. If it is not a vigorous one, he might succeed but only to the personal degree that he is capable. If it happens to be a rather truculent one, he may well find himself performing in a manner which will bring gasps of horror to his acquaintances and even louder gasps from his *super ego*. There, then is born your conflict. It is overcome on one side or the other, depending upon which side of the scales the weight falls. When reduced to intelligible terms, stripped of the floss and mush of gabbling idiots trying to silk purse the sow's ear, it comes out almost mathematically and is understandable unless you stand in fear of the disintegration of the universe, a most egocentric attitude."

"I have progressed," I repeated, "and I should like to thank you from the bottom of my heart for this enlightening and stimulating talk. You did not tell me a single thing I did not already know, but as you know, one often finds it impossible to use that knowledge. To hear it spoken in a voice of authority lends weight to personal convictions. Let me assure you sir, you have helped me more than you know. Actually, there have been a number of people who have helped and an odder assortment you could hardly imagine. An aunt of mine who has lived and has loved it. A private detective, who has no illusions about humanity and for that reason is probably more tolerant of it. A Negro woman who is a real friend, who saw with peculiar penetration what was happening and strove to do her part to make it right. A college girl who like many of her sisters, has wisdom beyond her years, not because of the educational system, but in spite of it. A woman, Lenthe, of whom I spoke, who in spite of leaving me in a manner which I have not yet understood, gave real meaning to many things which had escaped me. Another colored girl who with astounding intelligence and insight saw through me, felt sorry for me because of her immense kindness of heart, stimulated me by her strange beauty and gave me her body as solace. All these wonderful people have helped and yet not one did so by constraint or the urge of any conscience. They did so because they are fundamentally kind and sympathetic. I received from them what I could never have ordered or demanded as. my right. I had no right and no call upon their time or kindness and yet they gave it, without once mentioning my immortal soul or offering me salvation. All they did was give my true self an opportunity to walk alone. They offered to strike off the shackles and let me walk free and to that end they have toiled. Talking with you was one of the last needed strokes. There is much still to learn, but I believe I can now approach learning with the proper perspective without fear, the fear that caused me to assign a fact to oblivion if it offended my early training. I did not deny it, I just refused to allow it to take form. With my training, I could not say it didn't exist, but I could draw the curtain and refuse to let it touch me. I shall not attempt to burden you with thanks because I feel that you can see what your talk has meant to me."

His smile was a benediction. "Of course, my son. I listen to thanks respectfully because my people feel that if they make them strong enough they have in some way repaid me and I let them think so. They cannot all expect to know that achievement makes their thanks almost a bore. Usually, I know if I have done good and the knowledge is enough."

I walked down Bourbon Street toward Slim Jim's, feeling like no man not having lived through my own sensational rebirth could possibly imagine. I was going to get drunk, objectively and with premeditation.

CHAPTER ELEVEN

SHADOW AND SUBSTANCE

THE next day, in spite of my previous experience in the Roosevelt lobby, I bent my footsteps in the direction of Canal Street, knowing subconsciously that I'd end up somewhere near the hotel, but telling myself the reason was a need for a particular brand of cigarettes. The fact that I do not like cigarettes, and the consideration that they could have been purchased at any bar, restaurant, or grocery store, did not occur to me.

I hovered about the Baronne Street entrance trying to make myself as inconspicuous as possible behind a newspaper. I then went around to the other entrance and did more surreptitious hovering; neither of these maneuvers produced anything more than the usual complement of comers and goers, all intent upon their own business. Beneath the edge of the newspaper, I saw something that was vaguely familiar so I took a better look. A pair of shoes worn by someone standing some twenty feet away, assiduously studying a newspaper similar to mine. I pondered the matter for some time, wondering why these particular shoes should ring the bell of memory. Then, it struck me like a dash of cold water, that I had seen the same shoes while I shadowed the Baronne Street entrance. They were ordinary shoes, in an architectural sense, with only a particularly repellent shade of brown to distinguish them. In some manner they must have offended my senses and impressed my subconscious while I was not consciously aware of the occurrence. I watched the man for a while but he kept his attention riveted to the paper and not once did he glance in my direction.

I shall now, I thought, put this thing to a test. After a yawn, which I strove to make casual, I walked back to Canal Street and then down Baronne again, taking my post in the same place as before. There he was again, although I didn't see him come. He was standing, his back against a lamp post, perusing the paper as before. Suddenly a red flare of rage arose in me. I was being shadowed and I not only resented it but I wondered for what purpose it was being done. I had done nothing to warrant such close surveillance. With a gesture of decision, I dropped my paper in a refuse can and walked into a nearby tobacconist's shop where there were public telephones. Closing the booth, I dropped in a coin and dialed Slim Jim's place, wondering if he'd be able to aid me. Outside the booth I saw Brown Shoes attempting to get a booth next to me. As they were both filled, he could only dance impotently about and hope that one or the other occupants would depart. Jim, himself, answered the phone.

"What would you do, Jim, if you knew you were being followed?"

Jim chuckled. "I'd bushwhack the stinker, beat the hell out of him, then make him tell me why he was tailin' me ... You bein' followed?"

I told him I was. "You're a friend of mine, aren't you Jim?"

"Try me," he retorted succinctly.

"Very well. I have an idea that might work." I told him in a few words what it was.

"Sounds good to me, Prof, and you can count on this end. Be watchin' for you."

Ten minutes later, I dismounted from a cab and walked casually into Jim's place, noticing that a cab had stopped further down the street and a man was getting out of it. This I saw from the corner of my eye and I continued walking without turning my head. I walked toward the open end of the bar nearest the bandstand where Jim awaited me with a deceptive dullness in his eyes. I could tell that he was actually very alert.

"Where?" he asked as I walked up.

"Close behind!" I muttered. "What's the pitch?" I felt very gangsterish and wicked.

"Right here under me," muttered Jim in return, "is a trap door leading to the liquor celler. You clip 'im with one of them joojoos and we'll slide 'im through this door. Then you'll have a chance for chat and a little persuasion if he begs for it. I got all the seats occupied 'cept the last two. You take the next to the last and he'll have to take the last … Know you're on to 'im?"

I shook my head. "I don't think so."

"Okay, set down and I'll make you a Collins."

I sat but instead of feeling nervous, I was steady as a rock, relaxed, a feeling of cold inflexible purpose suffusing me. The man must have looked about a bit before he came in or was waiting for a purpose because I had my Collins and had taken a sip before he sat beside me. I remained still for a moment then took a flashing glance at his shoes. It was he! I sat for a while, sipping my Collins while the man drank a Coca-Cola, ignoring me as completely as though I had been in the next county … I mean parish.

Suddenly I turned around on my seat and gripped him by the shoulder. Exerting all my strength, I turned him forcibly about.

"I should like to know why you are following me," I said in chill tones.

"Get your hand offa me," he growled, "and who said I was following you?"

"I saw you at one entrance of the hotel, at the other, in the tobacco store and now here. I would like to know why and for whom are you working?"

Our voices had been kept low and no one seemed to notice what was occurring. He sneered and struck my hand from his shoulder.

"People in hell," he jeered, "would like a nice plate of orange sherbet."

I stood and he did too, which was what I wanted. In a flash, I jabbed him just beneath the sternum with the fingers of my right hand extended stiffly. If they strike the proper place, it can be a most demoralizing blow. My aim was excellent and he groaned and bent over which I had also planned that he do. I landed a sharp chop over his medulla, catching him as he fell forward. In a flash, Jim and I slid him around the bar, through the trap door and down the chute which was used for disposing of cases of empty beer bottles.

Jim plucked at my arm as I prepared to follow. "Go through that there curtain to the left of the bandstand, Prof. Keep left and you'll see a flight of steps to the cellar. Make all the racket you want ... I'll put a nickel in the juke box."

I doubt that anyone comprehended what had happened, although several saw us dispose of the man and were looking at us curiously. Such is the power of absorption in one's own business, and since the thing had been done quietly, there was no uproar.

When I arrived in the cellar, the man was sitting on a case of beer, holding his head.

I walked very close before he looked up. He snarled and reached beneath his left armpit but I was expecting some such move. I delivered a kick which struck accurately just below the patella, which might have broken his knee had he been standing. As it was, it fetched a yell from him and he grabbed the injured member with both hands.

"You broke it!" he gasped while I removed the gun from him and held it with what I'm sure must have been the ultimate in awkwardness.

"In that event," I said crisply, "my intentions were fulfilled. Now you have one good knee and one bad one. Would you like to be injured for life?"

He glared at me, his eyes red with rage. "How would you like to go to hell?"

"I can see no object in such a journey. If, perchance, you think I'm jesting when I ask these questions, you are in error. I should not like to break your remaining means of locomotion."

"I get you, bud," he grated, still holding his injured knee.

"I arranged this little party," I told him severely, "to the end that I should learn why you are following me. Either you answer my questions or I shall be forced to injure you further."

Suddenly he reached out and caught my left foot, tugging backward with all his strength. He was quick and his maneuver successful, but he was not aware that I too was quick and had hairtrigger coordination. Even as he jerked on my foot, I swung my arms viciously to take the weight off my feet and kicked him full in the face with my right heel, falling backward with a crash on a stack of empty beer bottles, upsetting them and sending up a hideous clatter. My shadow was *hors de combat* as I had known from the terrific jar which flashed up my leg that he would be. It is no small matter to get kicked in the face, especially in the particular manner with which I delivered my pedal blow. The results were more than gratifying. A slit showed at the top of the chute.

"Was that you or him, Prof?" hissed Jim from the opening.

"It was both of us," I said, dusting myself off. "I, however, am all right. He, on the other hand, due to his own truculence, is now somewhat the worse for his efforts."

I could hear Jim's chuckle. "That's what I figgered."

The trap closed and we were alone again. I broke the neck from a bottle of beer, pouring it unceremoniously over the man's face and for the first time I noticed that he was quite a husky individual. He was short and stocky, but he must have weighed nearly two hundred pounds, I decided, when I tried to move him. After some minutes, he regained consciousness and sat up groggily. He had lost all his front teeth, both upper and lower and his lips were a pulpy horror. He let go a hollow groan and vomited voluminously on the floor. I grew somewhat faint and had to sit on a nearby case of empty bottles while my stomach threatened to join his in protest. I gritted my teeth and fed myself another dose of rage as a therapeutic measure. It worked well and again I approached him, catching him by the hair, forcing his head back and looking into his eyes.

"Are you prepared to tell me what I want to know?"

His eyes were glazed with pain as he was suffering tortures, but his first mumbling words surprised me somewhat. "How'd you do it?"

"The details of my tactics are of no moment," I said with exasperation. "In just three seconds I'm going to attack you again. I assure you that this time not even a close relative will recognize you when I'm through."

Even in pain and under threat, the fellow retained his sense of humor. Feeling of his lips, he said gingerly, "Wouldn't none of 'em recognize me now. I guess there must be a limit to what a man owes a job that pays in just plain money. What do you want to know?"

"Who hired you?"

"Gent name of Palmar ... lives at the hotel."

"What were your instructions?"

"He described you and told me to keep an eye on you if you showed up, to see if you and his wife was meeting any place." He groaned and spat out a mouthfull of blood, freckled with bits of enamel.

"Why does he want to know that?"

He frowned heavily. "You kiddin'? Why wouldn't a man want to know if his wife was cheatin' on him?"

"That is not the reason and you know it. One second ..."

"Okay, chum, you win. He wants to get some dope on her so he can block any divorce action she might start. If she kicks him out with a pay-off, he stands to lose a lotta jack. She offered fifty G's but he's got his eye on a lot more."

"He is a cheap villainous lout, a perfect cad … a bounder!" I burst out, clenching my fists, feeling murderous.

The man looked at me quietly. "That's new brand of cussin', mister. I don't believe I ever heard it before."

I flushed and calmed somewhat. Now that it had all happened, I felt ill and ashamed of myself. After all, the man was working for a living, following the orders of his employer. I felt repentant and inclined to do something for him.

"Go to a good doctor and have your lips treated," I said gently. "When they're well, find the best dentist you can and get those teeth replaced and have both bills sent to me. I shall be glad to pay any expense you may incur in having the damage repaired. I would not like it, however, if you go back and report to Palmar. Are you with an agency or do you work alone?"

He shrugged helplessly. "First job I've had in a month. I work alone and do leg jobs on assignment. I ain't officially affiliated with any agency."

"That is better," I said. "Some agencies have ethics which I'm afraid we would have to break or at the least, bruise badly."

"After this," he said dismally, "I wouldn't dare face Palmar. I think I know where he got his busted arm now."

"You are quite correct. I intend to dispose of Palmar in some manner, the exact nature of which I have not yet decided. He is beginning to irk me."

The man looked at me for awhile and shook his head. "I can't make you out, mister, but I'll say this, you shoot square."

"I'm sorry I had to brutalize you," I said. "I would have preferred it some cleaner way, but you allowed me no alternative. I harbor no ill will and I hope you will feel the same way. Naturally you feel resentful that I had to resort to such tactics. However, I repeat, I shall be delighted to defray any expenses incident to repairs on your teeth and face. What was Palmar paying you?"

"Twenty-five a day and expenses. He ain't paid me anything yet."

I took out three twenties and handed them to him. "I hope you'll consider this as payment and, if you wish, I shall speak to a friend of mine who is a private detective with the object of securing you further employment in the future."

"Who is he?" asked the man suspiciously.

"A Mr. Danglos. He has an office in the Pere Marquette Building."

"Yeah?" he ejaculated. "He's high-class. He's got a reputation all over the country that even Pinkerton could use. In fact, he's taken on some jobs that Pinkerton's would have liked for themselves."

This was news. I didn't know that Dang was so well known.

"Are you satisfied with my propositions?"

"That's right, mister. I'm sore as hell, but mostly at myself. I ain't made a mistake like this in a long time."

I took out a card and scribbled my address on it. "Have the bills sent here," I said. "Would you like a drink before you go?"

"I'll try," he said, "but it'll probably burn me up."

I assisted him up the steps and out into the bar. He held a bloody handkerchief over his face as he walked unsteadily to the bar and sat on a stool. He managed to get a double portion of bourbon down with the aid of a straw, thoughtfully provided by Jim. He then left to have his face attended to.

I sat silently for a while, sipping at a Collins, waiting till Jim got through serving a new freshet of customers. Eventually, he came back and leaned on the bar in front of me.

"You kick the everlastin' tripe out of people and then buy 'em drinks. You been doin' that long?" Jim laughed. "You beat anything I ever saw, Prof, and let me tell you that was the neatest job I ever seen … what you done on him. It was even better than the one you pulled on that grumpy taxi driver."

"And the next day," I put in, "he performed a signal service for me. You see, such an attitude has its rewards."

"That's right," he agreed readily, "but there ain't many people what can rule themselves to that point. Most of 'em woulda let me throw that taxi driver out on his ear and enjoyed it. You got guts, Prof... and savvy too."

He was frankly admiring and I'm afraid I became pink about the cheeks. It was pleasant, though, to hear him say such kind things and being lost in the enjoyment of them, I missed his first hiss and he had to tug at my sleeve. Even then, I didn't understand. When finally I saw that he was trying to convey a subtle message to me, I turned around to see what he was trying to indicate with his eyes, elbows, and shoulders and looked full into Lenthe's face.

I was shocked into a numbing paralysis. The sight threw me into such a pitiable state of confusion that I could only sit and stare at her. Her face was twice as lovely as before and her great soft eyes were damp with unshed tears. I felt utterly slain, thrown off my balance and all the misery and hurt I had suffered now came back with a rush, so much so that it cleared my mind somewhat and raised a knot of galling resentment in my throat.

"Oh my darling, what have I done to you?" she whimpered softly, setting my pulses to hammering, my mind veering crazily.

A beelzebub sat on my shoulder and whispered in my ear. 'The queen has deigned to notice you again, victim. She feeds you sweetness then cuts you dead.' I suppose too many things had happened at once because I felt myself choke with hurt and furious resentment. She had embarrassed me, caused me hours of heartache, then spoken coldly to me as to a stranger. Tears of self-pity and that sweet stifling sensation which one feels when being eaten by blind stubbornness began to take hold of me. I drew back and my eyes narrowed. I put my Collins carefully on the bar and stood.

"Madame," I said, making my voice as cold and impersonal as I possibly could, "you have evidently made a mistake. I never saw you before in my life." Having spoken, and riding the first wave of a very hollow triumph, I walked around her and started for the door.

She ran after me, catching my arm. "Please, Thomas, won't you listen to me?"

I turned and forcibly removed her hand from my sleeve. "You're being ridiculous," I said with meticulous sarcasm, "and you may tell Palmar for me that if he assigns more men to watch me, I'll mail them to him in bits. Now, if you don't mind, I have business elsewhere and though I've never struck a pretty woman, and you are pretty in a blowsy, cheap sort of way, I shall be forced to take harsh measures if you accost me again."

The way she fell back, her eyes dark with pain, one might have thought I had struck her. I went through the door with that overpowering sense of having won the round which would bury me, choking with pain, blind with tears and girded with the false armor of righteousness, knowing that right or wrong, I had made a cyclopean ass of myself. Now there is a reaction, the study of which might prove edifying. Why do men and women do it? Had she come to me as she appeared the day in the hotel, I would have been ready to beg her forgiveness on bended knee. But because she approached me with a penitent air, I, instead of accepting the situation and saving myself the embarrassment of prostrating myself before her, chose to become sensitive and antagonistic, to whip my vanity into the full flush of betrayal, the results of which were as I have related.

CHAPTER TWELVE
LIPS THAT TOUCH LIQUOR

STUMBLED into my apartment and proceeded to get steaming drunk on whiskey and water, as disgusting a concoction as ever smote the palate of man. Valentine pleaded with me till she wore herself out, then sank into a nearby chair and wept bitterly. This filled me to the brim with that variety of masochistic delight with which men often flagellate themselves, enjoying causing pain to others while causing even more to themselves. I apparently passed out cold some time between dark and midnight because when I woke I was alone, still drunk, sick, miserable, and cold. I went to the bathroom and vomited till I had nothing left to bring up. Still, I continued to gag violently, bringing forth a drool of bitter bubbles and going blind from the effort. Dripping with sweat and sicker than I ever remember being in my life, I reeled into the bedroom and collapsed on the bed.

I thought about Lenthe and wept bitterly into a pillow smeared with slimy emesis. I was in much too wretched a state to care. After a time, I fell asleep from sheer physical exhaustion.

The next morning, Valentine fixed me a breakfast which I couldn't eat. I'm sure it was delicious but the thought of food turned my stomach. I was in such acute misery that I yelled viciously at her to leave me alone when she tried to talk to me and I went into the living room to collapse on the couch.

Some time later, Danglos came over, summoned doubt-lessly by Valentine, who saw she couldn't do anything with me. I divined, too, that Lenthe had seen him.

"And how is my prize porker this lovely Sunday morning?" he gobbled as he walked in.

I turned my face to the wall and groaned.

"Men who do that," he said lugubriously, "are just before dying, so 'tis said in the southland."

I did not speak, so he took a seat.

"I thought you were all repentant and ready to kiss her feet and yet, when you see her, you buckle on your pride and sweep haughtily from the room with bitter recriminations on your lips. I ask you, is that the mark of an educated man?"

I sat up and eyed him feverishly. "I saw her once and she affected not to have seen me before. I called her and she cut me dead, hanging up in my ear. When it pleased her, she came back yelping some saccharine muck about 'Darling, what have I done to you.' I suppose I'm some goddamned little puppy who sits around and waits till the table is swept so that he might catch a crumb or two. Thank you, I don't care for any."

Dang whistled to himself for a moment, looking out of the window. "You have it all figured out, son. Just like I did. Your armor is puncture-proof and righteousness rideth by thy side, or around your neck ... same difference. When you've drunk your-self into a state of helpless coma and are sick unto death, maybe you'll get some sense. I didn't, but then, I'm a lot dumber than you."

I lost my temper and felt like hurting someone again. "If you're quite through," I said, "kindly go about your business, if you have any. For past services you may send me a bill which I shall honor immediately. I shall have no further need of your invaluable assistance."

He nodded affably. "If this wasn't so familiar, the impact would sting more. Be assured, however, that all will be well or

Thomas McBride Tallant will occupy a slab in the morgue with Aunt Cam snuffling by, saying 'poor boy'."

"Your humor provides me with a severe and highly localized pain," I said. "I repeat, your absence is preferable to your company. That applies as of now and unto infinity."

"Infinity is an admission of futility," said Dang grinning infuriatingly. "Upon the inability to place a limit one uses the word infinity."

"I used it to indicate the entire lack of a limit," I said and deliberately stretched out on the couch, turning my back on him.

He left, whistling as cheerfully as if I had given him a drink and my unqualified blessing. I must have slept again for when I next was conscious of anything, the sun was at its zenith and I felt somewhat hungry. Valentine had gone, a matter which drove me into a rage. I went in and drank a glass of milk which rebounded with such speed that I reached the bathroom with but inches to spare. I then lost my temper for good and for all. Going back to the kitchen, I got a bottle of whiskey and a pitcher of water. Feeling again as if I were hurting someone, myself really, although I had it aimed at some several nebulous enemies, I came back into the living room and poured myself a drink at which the fabled Paul Bunyan might have gagged. Nothing daunted, I drank it down like iced tea and was somewhat surprised that it did not also rebound. By now, I suppose my stomach was staggering and the blow dealt by that gargantuan drink was more than it could resist, so it meekly submitted. I began to feel better immediately and during the afternoon I sat brooding, thinking horrible thoughts concerning fiendish tortures, plottings, poisonings, and I don't recall what else. I continued drinking and when Valentine came in about five, I was ready for her. "I shall require you no longer," I blared harshly as she came into the living room. "Please take whatever possessions you may have here and depart. I never wish to see you again."

A free balloon of resentment began to choke me as I watched tears flood her eyes. "Oh, Mr. Tallant, what has come over you?"

"I am sick to death of people sticking their noses in my business," I told her. "You and that despicable woman, Lenthe and that gangling dangling Danglos. To hell with every last one of you. Get out of my sight!"

I hurled a glass at her which luckily missed and shattered itself against the far wall. For a moment, she stood watching me, tears streaming from her eyes, then she walked out of the house, her shoulders slumped in dejection. I fell with a thump to the bear rug and cried like a spoiled child, beating the thick fur with my fists and writhing in torment. After that storm was over, I sat weakly on the couch, picked up the bottle and finding I had thrown my glass away, I poured the remaining whiskey into the pitcher and drank it although the brew was too strong. I didn't mind greatly and about nine, I suppose, I passed out on the floor.

When I woke it was dark and I was chilled to the bone, still drunk, my throat burning with thirst. I reeled into the kitchen and with some effort made a pitcher of ice water, drinking from the pitcher till it seemed I'd burst. I should have known better, but my brain by this time functioned by reflex alone and the instant I put the pitcher down, the water came up with a force that shot it across the breakfast table and against the far wall. I didn't even have time to rise from the chair. I dropped my head on my arms and shuddered violently as though with a chill.

I went to sleep in this position and woke up just as dawn was breaking—weak, cold, with every muscle in my body protesting vehemently. When I tried to get to the bedroom, I fell flat after about three steps. I had to crawl the rest of the way and when I reached the bed, I found I didn't have enough strength to get into it.

With something like coherent thought, I knew that I must have nourishment or I'd die. I crawled back to the kitchen and opened the ice box, taking out a bottle of milk. I drank thirstily, feeling better instantly. I even managed, through the help of the milk, although it hadn't actually been down long enough to act and the help was probably psychological, to get to my feet and totter to the bedroom. I fell across the bed and lay like a dead man for a long time. Conscious, if the term is used loosely, but without a thought of any kind. Then without warning, the milk decided it had been down long enough and came up. I was so weak and dispirited that I didn't even bother to turn my head to allow it to spill on the floor, most of it going on the bed. Remembering that the day before, the whiskey had stayed down when nothing else would, I went into the kitchen and found the last bottle and made a powerful drink which I tossed down with all the ease of Danglos. It stimulated and refreshed me and I even had the industry to carry the bottle and pitcher into the living room where I placed them on the coffee table and made another drink.

I drank that and began to feel transcendental. I threw a towering rage individually and collectively at everyone I knew, including Miss Cannon, who was entirely innocent of any recent happenings. I tore up a table lamp and shattered a marble figurine to bits on the floor. I stood before the mirror and declaimed mightily, calling down all manner of evils on my enemies with devasting rhetoric, delivering crushing broadsides of sterling logic, peppered with acidulous sarcasm. I was wonderful! I surpassed verbally anything I had ever said before. In the mirror, my face was lit with triumph and carried the sneer of superb arrogance that used to mark the face of Il Duce when he spoke; although, I forgot at the moment that the look invariably sent the spectators into stitches. I pictured myself as a friendless Napoleon, beset on all sides by traitors and enemies of every stripe, all waiting till the back should bend or the eye should cloud to swoop down and rend me with their talons...talons, they all had talons like eagles—claws, razor sharp, ready to pierce the hides of the weak and stupid. And who was weak and stupid? Not I! I smote myself in the chest with such force that I coughed violently for a considerable time, so I took another drink. The enemy was drawing closer because I could hear the sounds of the drums … drums … drums. My head seemed filled with them and through it all I could hear the rumble of artillery and the shrill of fifes. Steps … steps … steps. Steps on my threshold and hands fumbling with the latch.

I got up and started toward the door. I would not be caught unawares as they hoped I would. The moment the door opened, I would launch my attack into the valley of death. The door opened and I sprang like a wild thing. I made contact and suddenly excruciating pain shot through my shoulder and I had a sensation of flying, then a shuddering crash which seemed to pulverize every bone in my body, then peace … calm, puffy, rubbery peace.

Through the fog of delicious peace, I heard a voice say, "Ye gods, Senior, take away three years and I could say, this is where I came in!"

Then I knew nothing, a condition which I seemed to have been occupying for a long time. I know only because I was told that I stayed out a day and that a doctor came and fed me things through a vein, slot things into my arms and in general disported himself with my unresisting body.

When next I opened my eyes, I was weak as no kitten that ever was born could have been, else he'd never have reached cathood. I felt no pain because I felt nothing. I had sensations akin to that of a lost thought wandering around, searching for a mind. A female, whom I did not know, came and stood at the foot of my bed. Her skin was a rich tan and her eyes cold, sea blue. She was an amazon of a creature, standing nearly six feet, and constructed along lines that would have delighted a master sculptor. She wore clothes that showed her figure to an advantage, but there was a forbidding air about her that made me want to pull the cover over my head, something for which I didn't have the strength.

"Greetings, bird brain," she said with easy inelegance. "I see you have decided not to die. What a pity! We had such a lovely packing box all ready to sink you in. We picked it up in an alley."

I felt a quiver of revulsion flit over me. What a macabre thought!

"We have two alternatives. We feed you and run the risk of all sorts of bizarre eventualities or we just let you lay there and dwindle away. It wouldn't be much of a dwindle because you are so far along the road already. Actually, it would be a lot of trouble for everyone concerned to bring you back to life, so I think the best thing is to let you go ahead and dwindle the other ten inches and have done with it."

A man appeared at her back, a tall man with shoulders nearly as wide as the door and arms like oaken posts. His face was kindly and reserved with lines of tremendous strength of character. His handsome lips moved in a smile.

"Quit badgering him," he ordered. "Do you think he can eat?"

"Shut up!" she retorted with authority. "I'm giving him a pretty picture of himself. This place still smells of puke, which irritates me." Then the hard carven planes of her face softened. "Think you can eat, Tommy?"

"Who are you?" I croaked.

"I'm Sundown Roland and this brute here is my husband."

My mind appeared to be working well because in a flash there came back to me what Dang had said about her: "The best friend I have in the world ... extraordinary woman." I recalled the voice saying this was where she came in as I lay in a semi-conscious condition on the living room floor.

"I attacked you when you came, didn't I?"

She smiled and I felt like I had taken a drink. Her face lit up, her teeth flashing against the rich tan of her skin.

"You could call it that. I had to toss you a little just as I did Dang a few years ago. It was nothing."

I tried to move and decided that maybe to her it was nothing, but to me it had almost been the end. I felt as though every muscle had been crushed between stones and my bones powdered. As long as I expended no effort, I felt no pain, but the slightest move made me almost faint.

"Think you could eat something?" she asked again, and the knife edge had gone from her voice.

"I don't know ... maybe. Nothing heavy."

They left me and came back after a while with a small portion of egg, whipped up in cream. I got it down and my stomach set up such a clamor that it could be heard growling and chuckling twenty feet away. All that day they fed me in small amounts every hour or so, graduating from liquid to a tasty cornmeal gruel flavored with ham stock. At nightfall, I took a slice of toast and a soft-boiled egg. Later that night, I was given two pieces of toast and a cup of tea. An hour later, I had a small glass of water and a yellow capsule which put me to sleep in a matter of minutes.

CHAPTER THIRTEEN
MORNING BECOMES ELECTRIC

AWOKE the next morning with the sun slanting into my window, distributing a cheery golden glow. I didn't feel as sore as I had the day before and I felt I could eat a pig of respectable size, hair, hide, and bones. Valentine came to the room and stood in the doorway. At the sight of her, I went weak with remorse, my eyes overflowing with tears. She rushed to the bedside and sank beside it.

"Oh, Mr. Tallant, I'm so glad you're all right. I almost died before Mr. Danglos would do anything. He said you'd have to get good and drunk before anyone could do anything for you."

"I'm bitterly sorry I spoke as I did to you, Valentine. You, of all people, who stood by me and helped in every way you could and I repaid by reviling you and ordering—"

She put her hand over my mouth. "Be quiet," she ordered, "or you'll get no breakfast or anything else. Are you hungry?"

"Starving!" I said. "What can I have?"

"Mrs. Roland said you could have oatmeal and cream with two or three slices of toast. I'm to feed you in small amounts today as fast as you get hungry. Oatmeal, soft-boiled eggs, grits, toast, coffee or tea."

"Well, let's get started. I'm caving in."

Valentine laughed and went to fetch my breakfast. By that afternoon, I was in good enough condition to make a voyage to the living room unassisted, clad in pajamas and robe. About four o'clock, Mrs. Roland came in, bringing a youngster I took to be about two months old. It was a boy and a lustier infant I never saw. Where children of his age usually wallow helplessly about, their heads lolling aimlessly on their shoulders, this one managed his like a baby of six months. He gurgled and blew bubbles when he saw me and had none of the vacant stare usually seen in the eyes of infants. She placed him on the bear-rug where he immediately fell asleep.

"I feel that mere spoken thanks would be poor repayment for your help, Mrs. Roland," I began, but she cut me off.

"Save it," she said crisply. "Dang called us because I had yanked him through just such an ordeal once and he thought I'd be good at it. My husband and I are birds of a feather and could, with justice, be called meddlers. We like to put things right. This newest bud on the family tree has kept me inactive for some time and I was feeling the need to flex my muscles. I didn't know that I'd have to flex them other than in the abstract, but I'm glad to see I've lost none of my timing."

"Where," I asked curiously, "did you learn Judo?"

"Marines. Charbonnet used me as a medicine ball for some time because I wouldn't squeak and yell quits. He taught me quite a lot and I learned plenty from Colonel Biddle."

"I recall seeing Colonel Biddle once," I said enthusiastically. "I was amazed that a man of his age could handle himself so well."

"You'd have been really amazed if he ever got his hands on you," she said dryly. "I weighed a hundred and thirty-five pounds when I was in the Bams and on exhibition he used to toss me like a sack of hay and he never told us to play dead. We could resist if we wanted to, but we knew better."

I sighed. This strong vital woman with her searching blue eyes and magnificent body with its extraordinary musculature made me feel positively crotchety.

She whacked me across the face with her eyes with such force that I winced. "Tommy, it is the lot of man that he be four-fifths ass at some time during his life. But it is not intelligent to remain one. How do you feel now about Lenthe?"

I shuddered beneath the blow. "If it would do any good, I'd crawl a mile in the mud to fall at her feet. If you are wondering whether I've learned my lesson, the answer is an emphatic yes. I think I have remained your four-fifths part of an ass longer than most and I derive nothing from the memory but a desire to hide under the bed."

Her eyes grew gentle and understanding. "I know, Tommy." Her voice caressed and had a curiously rich note. "We get thrown for losses by things which, after they are all over, seem the pinnacle of stupidity. Still, recrimination is unproductive and a waste of time and energy. The sooner forgotten, the better. Lenthe was wrong in a great many ways and she's brave enough to admit it, but she's young and unhappy, Tommy. It was a blow when her father left her all bound up in pitfalls, snares, time limits, and I don't know what all. She took what seemed to be the easiest way and she could not be expected to know it would turn out badly. Lieutenant Pizzo has traced the man and though he has been on trial several times for various offenses, he has never been convicted and we can't remove him on the strength of his record although we are morally certain that he's a creep. However, such a minor obstacle is nothing to men like my husband and his friend Edward Toussaint, better known as Edwa."

"I met Mr. Toussaint one night at Dang's," I said. "He impressed me as a man of sudden violent action."

"I salute your impression," she said laughing. "Your instincts were on the ball. Pitt, my husband, is a man who studies and ponders, but Edwa prefers to wade in and tear up the landscape with both fists swinging. They have a proposition to make."

"I refused Mr. Toussaint's kind offer before," I said, "but much has happened since to change my way of thinking. I shall eagerly await their proposition."

"And upon the completion of that, you'll be willing to do something about Lenthe?"

I nodded vigorously. "If, by that time, she has not decided that I'm unworthy of her attentions."

"I think I can safely predict a favorable reaction from her," she said confidently, scooping her infant from the floor like a rag doll. She threw him over her shoulder, from which perch he peered at me and grinned toothlessly. "They'll be over tonight after they've had dinner and bedded it down with brandy. They'll tell you what they have on their minds."

They came in after dinner, Dang, Roland, Toussaint, and their wives. Toussaint and Roland constituted a race of men which I'm sure could hardly have been equaled for sheer power. Together they must have weighed close to a quarter of a ton and walked with that feral grace which suggests speed as well as strength, a rare and devastating combination when interpreted in terms of physical violence. I was afraid Toussaint, in his bubbling ebullience, would smite me on the back and I knew if he did the blow would probably render me unconscious. He respected my low condition, however, and didn't even break my hand when he shook it.

The infant was deposited unprotesting upon the rug by Edwa. After a period during which he talked chaffingly to the child and importuned him to say Uncle Edwa innumerable times, he took a chair and left him to his own devices which consisted principally of grinning impartially at everyone and trying to devour his fist. After a time, in spite of the thundering laughs of Toussaint, he went placidly to sleep.

"Now, Thomas," said Toussaint, raising his hand to strike and thinking better of it, "I understand you're considering a rehearing on the subject of what to do with friend Palmar."

"I am indeed. I feel that much of the trouble I've caused you might have been avoided if I had listened in the first place."

"Doubtless," he agreed, "doubtless, however, error is the lot of mankind. I made one once myself."

"Here we go again!" groaned Angelique, Toussaint's wife.

"The mistake was not yours," said Roland soberly, "but your parents'. They knew not what they did and therefore may be forgiven, but not excused."

"I ignore you," snapped Edwa.

"Palpably a maneuver to gain time to think," said Roland placidly, "with little thought to the lack of materials, a modicum of which is necessary to the production of mental processes."

"Knock it off!" ordered Sunny, grinning at the antics of Toussaint and her husband.

"Don't you two ever get weary of all this fencing? Thomas is waiting to know what you have cooked up."

Toussaint hitched his chair around and faced me. "There are any number of possibilities to choose from, the choice being dictated by several things like the availability of the man, his personality and things of that sort. We could kidnap him and put him in the iron maiden, after whose embrace he'd be glad to agree with anything we suggested."

"I ... er ... is there to be physical coercion?" I felt a bit ill.

"Not of the violent sort. There are too many mild, but impressive methods at hand."

Danglos spoke up. "There are, as he says, many mild means, but ask him how many times he ever used them."

Edwa grinned satanically. "When in Rome ... we use the sort of tactics which seem to fit the occasion."

"Like that rattlesnake with which you scared the daylights out of one of Dutch Samothrace's men."

"That particular hood was lucky that his bones were all intact when we finished," said Roland with deadly seriousness.

I learned subsequently that this Dutch individual had been a gambler and at the time they quizzed the man in question, Miss Smith, now Roland, was a kidnap victim.

"Palmar," continued Edwa, "lives in the Roosevelt, is that right?"

"That is correct. He and Lenthe stay in separate rooms."

They laughed at my vehemence which discomfited me considerably as I hadn't realized I had spoken so energetically.

Roland looked at the ceiling meditatively. "What we want is some good evidence that will make a divorce easy for Lenthe."

"I've got that all figured out," said Edwa smugly. "What I want now is someone to tell me how to get the guy out of the place."

"I may be able to help there," I said, sitting up excitedly. "I had a little exercise with a detective whom he had detailed to watch me and although I was forced to brutalize him somewhat, we parted on good terms. I think this man might be bribed to place a call which would bring the man pell-mell, if at the same time Lenthe was absent from the hotel."

"I'll take the job of securing Lenthe's cooperation," said Sunny.

Now I could understand what Dang meant when he said that it was no disloyalty to Adrienne to call Sunny an extraordinary woman. I could see that Lenthe would cooperate whether it suited her fancy or not.

CHAPTER FOURTEEN

AFTERNOON TEA

SINCE I was not a debilitated dipsomaniac, I recovered quickly from my first brush with the cup, and the next day, though I felt a little weak in the knees, I dressed and went out for a stroll. At noon, I was famished and ate a good meal. After eating, I felt I was ready to perform any and all strategic moves that might be asked of me. My first job was to locate and negotiate with the detective. With the help of Jim, I succeeded, and that afternoon we rented a cheap little place down near the river which was to be the scene of our operations.

The time set was midafternoon on Thursday and the three of us went to the place and made ourselves comfortable, pending the arrival of the victim.

"I would prefer that there be as little physical violence as possible," I said as we sat in rickety chairs and looked at dank walls.

Toussaint erupted in a bellow of laughter and Roland smiled. "From what Dang tells us," said the former, "you aren't too bad in a mixup yourself."

I said with dignity, "A man cannot allow himself to become a foot mat."

"If things work the way we intend," said Roland reassuringly, "there will be little, if any, violence. To begin with, the man has a broken arm and is in no condition to run the risk of manhandling."

Toussaint looked at a huge, stainless steel wristwatch which against the background of his thick, hairy arm appeared to be of normal size. "It is ten minutes to the hour," he mused. "If I was Palmar with his mind sown thick with suspicion from his rich past, I'd be a mite leery if I were told to report to a place like this. Whew, I can smell the fish market from here. I'm going out and lurk in alleys so if he changes his mind at the last moment, I'll be there to change it back for him."

He left and we sat quietly, though I must admit, I was nervous. Roland might not have had a nerve in his great body as he relaxed in the chair, puffing on a cigarette. Ten minutes passed, then ten more, and I felt as if I'd burst something if things did not begin to happen. Then came a knock on the rickety back door. With a bound, that for speed and grace was almost unbelievable in a man of Roland's size, he came out of the chair and in two strides reached the door and opened it a crack. He grinned, opening wider to let in Toussaint, dragging a man by the scruff of the neck. It was Palmar, his face the color of putty from sheer funk. Toussaint shoved him into a chair with due regard for his injured arm and stood back to look at him. Palmar cowered, uttering a little throaty noise which did not seem to be a word or plea, just a frightened noise. The two men towered over him, crossing their mighty arms over their chests. They were dressed in nondescript blue pants and blue shirts of the seafaring man. Toussaint wore a blue cap at a devil-may-care angle. Together they made a forbidding pair.

"Son," began Toussaint with deceptive softness, "we don't like you."

"B—b—but, I've never done anything to you. I never saw you before. I don't get it ... what do you want?"

"You will be told all, son, in good time. First, to keep down any idea you may have of lying, I'll tell you something of yourself. Your name is Joseph Gruber. You were born in Diddle, Alabama, March the second, nineteen twenty-one. You have been arrested three times. Once as a suspect in a case involving a ten-year-old girl and twice for petty larceny. You were convicted on none of these charges. Then you discovered you had a certain attraction for women and cultivated good speech and manners so that you might pass as a gentleman. You happened to be handy when Lenthe Kensington needed a husband to get her inheritance, so she grabbed you. She tried to pay you off, but being a career man, you saw where you might do a lot better, so you refused to be bought off. I imagine that her refusal to sleep with you had something to do with it too, but nevertheless, we come to the main point in discussion. We are here to convince you that she's a poor wife for you. Get it?"

One could see that Palmar got it but he didn't like it a bit. "I'm her legal husband and I love her. I will not divorce her."

"And if we filled the bathtub with water and held your head under it, think that'd change your mind?"

Palmar was not without courage for all his ratty appearance. "It might verbally, but it takes a year here in Louisiana."

"There are places where it can be done quicker," said Roland. "Naturally, we have something in mind a great deal more solid than a verbal agreement. The point is, we must have your cooperation. Now, there is a girl who will agree to get into bed with you, attractively nude, and while you are both apparently in the clutch of passion, Edwa will snap a picture, several in fact. What is your answer?"

Palmar smiled thinly. "My reply is to tell both of you to go to hell ..."

Crack went Toussaint's hard palm on the man's face and I winced from the force of the blow as well as the lightninglike suddenness with which it was delivered. Palmar bleated like a kid from fear, not unmixed with pain, a slap being both unnerving and shocking.

"Regrets and all that sort of rot," breathed Toussaint, flexing his fingers that must have stung from the blow. "The point is, cousin, respect for peers as well as discipline must at all costs be preserved. Sorry, I'm sure. The pills, Pitt." Pittman is Roland's first name. Roland handed Edwa a green bottle filled with white tablets.

He shook them at Palmar. "These things are not poison. In fact, they'll make you feel so good that you'll want to attack me, although I wouldn't advise it. Now, do you take 'em or do I pretend you're a horse and stick them down your throat with my finger?"

"What are they?" asked Palmar sullenly.

"Benzedrine. Get a glass of water, Pitt."

Roland went into the bathroom and returned with a glass of water.

"Okay, pal, open your trap wide." Palmar resolutely kept his mouth closed. Edwa drew back his hand and made a feint at the man's face. Palmar tightened up all over and shut his eyes expecting to have his eyeballs jarred again but nothing happened. "Better take 'em son. It'll be a lot easier that way."

Palmar seemed to wilt, breathed deeply and opened his mouth. With a quick flexible flip of the wrist, his inquisitor flung the pills deep into his throat from whence he could not dislodge them, and a plop of water right behind them carried out the plan.

True to Toussaint's prediction, before darkness fell, Palmar, seeing that he wouldn't be subjected to any more violence, became affable. "You fellows might give me the prescription for that stuff when you finally see that I mean business. It packs a lift like nothing I ever saw."

Edwa nodded genially. "It does that, pal. Just so long as you don't take too much of it."

"Two tablets the dose?"

"Yep, it can be taken every four or five hours."

"What's the idea of giving it to me?"

"At the proper time, friend, all things will become crystal clear, that is, all the things we are interested in. Getting hungry?"

Palmar, who was feeling too well to be anything but agreeable said, "Yes, I could use a bite."

"Good … me too." Edwa rose to his feet and set his cap on his head. "I'll go to a nearby hashery and fetch a spread …." He stopped as the door opened to admit two powerful Negroes. They stood an easy six feet and their shoulders were broad, their chests deep and their waists narrow. Their arms had that soft, deceptive aspect that disappeared into long, sharply defined muscle whenever they tensed, a sign of keen condition.

"Well, what held you boys up?" asked Pitt.

"Moze ran out of gas on the way to the plantation," said one of the men, grinning.

"When he got to us he was almost crying he was so mad."

"Boys," said Edwa grinning, "this is Mr. Tallant. He's the one we're pulling this job for."

The Negroes bowed respectfully and murmured graceful words of greeting. I now noticed that they were almost identical in every respect, even to a most unnegroid scattering of freckles across their faces, the skin of which was noticeably red, a true red and not the publicized red of the Indian which is more of a tan or bronze.

Edwa sat down again. "Hardy, I'm tired from my endeavors. How's for you and Kent to walk half a block down the street and bring us back a spread of chow. You'll find a little restaurant there, a greasy spoon, I suppose … hold it. Damned if I want to corrode my guts with that stuff. Now that you two are here, we can go eat Jeff's cooking and heckle Dang. Palmar, you'll be eating beans and other gunk while I'm sitting down to a thick steak that has been seared, but not burned, running red in the middle, rubbed down with garlic—plus hot rolls, green salad, and that superb banana pie he makes. Coffee, brandy and cigars afterward … sorry, I'm sure."

Palmar swallowed noisily. "I'll try to survive," he said nastily.

"There'll come a time when you'll be in doubt, lad. You could save yourself a lot of needless nerve-shredding and us time and trouble."

Palmar leaped to his feet with astounding speed and jumped toward the door like a scared rabbit but Toussaint only smiled. As Palmar passed Hardy, the big Negro executed what looked like a dance step and hurled a thick hard leg at the flying feet of Palmar with devastating effect. I don't think I ever saw a man fall harder. The crash shook the building and a cloud of dust rose from the floor. It was some five minutes before he could collect himself sufficiently to rise and during that time we sat and watched him.

He finally got up and staggered back to his chair. "I've broken my arm all over again," he whimpered.

"Tough luck," growled Edwa. "You're goddam lucky you didn't break all over. I may have seen a harder fall, but brother, I never took one. Good work, Hardy."

I heaved a sigh. All this was pretty distasteful, particularly since none of the others seemed to be the least bothered. Toussaint seemed to enjoy the proceedings, one could not tell from Roland's placid face what he felt and the two Negroes were quiet, their faces controlled as carvings.

"We'll be shoving, Hardy," said Roland. "Come on out here and I'll give you the dope and you can tell Kent about it. Kent, you keep an eye on poison puss there."

Kent grinned and eased himself into a nearby chair. We all went outside where Roland gave Hardy instructions.

"When you think he's ripe, give us a buzz," he concluded. "As I say, all you have to do is to feed him those pills every four hours although the first few doses can be a lot farther apart. Keep him well fed and don't rough him unless you have to. You and Kent can sleep in shifts, but whatever you do, stay awake when you're on watch."

"Don't you worry, sir," said Hardy with quiet confidence.

We climbed in Toussaint's great car and rolled smoothly down Toulouse Street, then cut over to Royal and in a few minutes pulled up in front of Dang's apartment and, incidentally, my own. "We'll let you know when the coup is to be administered, Tom," said Toussaint, "so stay available."

"I shall not move from my quarters," I assured him.

CHAPTER FIFTEEN
PHOTO FINISH

VALENTINE had an excellent dinner awaiting me that night. Fried chicken, creamy fluffed potatoes, salad, green beans that due to her southern touch at last seemed to have acquired a taste. In some manner, she had filched a banana pie from Jeff, Danglos' cook. Whatever the state of my nerves, my appetite had regained and surpassed its former station and I'm afraid I made a pig of myself. After supper, while Valentine washed the dishes and put the kitchen in order, I sat in the living room and stared at the fire.

When she came in, she was prepared for the street, a raincoat over her arm. "Everything's all right, Mr. Tallant and unless you want something else …"

There was a knot of disappointment in my stomach. "You have a date tonight?"

"No, sir, but …" She seemed a little confused.

"Would you mind staying a while?" For a moment she looked at me then she fell to her knees and buried her face in my lap.

"I was afraid you had gotten tired of me." Her voice was muffled. I stroked the shining coils of her hair and the fine skin of her neck.

"I don't have any right to ask you to stay, really Valentine, I …"

She held her head up quickly. "Then you didn't believe me?"

With a rush of affection, I slid to the floor beside her and her smooth lips came under mine. She held to me like a starving person would clutch a loaf of bread.

"I was so afraid you might have meant something of what you said."

"I was crazy. I didn't know what I was saying. I wanted to hurt and when in that state, one hurts most the ones for whom he cares most. If I hadn't thought so much of you there would have been no compensation in hurting you. I would have ignored you entirely."

She was satisfied and cuddled close, letting a tired little sigh escape her. Our association had progressed to the point where she felt no need to make a show of modesty. The fact that her skirt was nearly to her waist, showing several inches of taut white nylon underthings occasioned her no concern, although I cannot say the same. My fingers touched the surface of her thigh like those of a textile buyer examining the weave of some exotic creation in satin. The leg drew up to meet my hand and her hot breath, coming faster, caressed my neck. Her hand sought my own, pressed it hard against her. A little crying whimper sounded in her throat, but I stifled it with a kiss.

It was an evening I shall long remember.

Valentine initiated me in secret ways of love I had never known existed. Where she had learned such things, I could not imagine. Her lovemaking was more fiery than ever, but had a sophistication far beyond that of, say, Josy—a subtlety that transcended even Lenthe's.

At one point she broke off our caresses to dance for me by the music of the radio. How unbearably exciting it was to watch her whirling, striding, shaking her tawny flesh in patterns at once utterly lascivious and utterly beautiful. The bare skin of her gleamed in the firelight. Her jet hair tossed. Her eyes flashed. When she passed close to me on her long and nimble legs, her dimpled hips quaking and shaking, I could no longer stand the torture and reached wildly for her thighs.

She permitted me to seize her. I was on my knees, overwhelmed by the dusky beauty of her and my own hot passion, my arms circling her hips. I buried my head in her soft, scented belly, kissed and cajoled the flesh with my lips and tongue. She remained standing, but bent back from the waist, arching her body, thrusting the belly and thighs of her forward to meet my blandishments.

"Oh," she gasped. "Oh, that's right. Now you are learning. Please me as I please you—oh—oh ...."

She writhed, wriggled, overcome by paroxysms of wildest, sheerest delight. With all my might and cunning I strove to do as she had asked—strove to please her. Suddenly she attained a shuddering height of ecstasy, sighed, than sank to her knees. But a moment later she rolled over on her back. "Oh, lover. Come to me. Kiss me and love me, you wonderful man—"

Thoroughly aroused, I obeyed her command. The sensation of my flesh slithering over her velvety skin drove me to frenzy. With every muscle in her sweet body, with every delicate curve and mound and hollow, she cunningly accommodated me. There followed a burst of bliss so explosive, yet so impossibly satisfying, that I shall never forget it.

Mouth to mouth, body to body, we waited for our breathing to return to normal, for our hearts to stop pounding. "My sweet Valentine," I whispered. "I love you. I love you. You are the one I should marry."

She laughed, and stroked my hair. "No, you don't love me and I don't love you. Not in the way you mean. We are good friends helping each other, and we admire each other's qualities, and together we are exploring beauty and passion. But do not be misled. We are not meant to marry. What would we do, spend the rest of our lives in bed?"

"No. Right here on the floor. On this white rug."

Again she laughed. "You're a darling to ask me. But it wouldn't work … Now, come one, love me some more!"

I proceeded to the fray. "How's that?"

"You're learning," she admitted. "You're learning all the time. You have already acquired the secret of successful love-making—which is to devote yourself to pleasing your partner, not yourself, and in this way, miraculously, doubling your own degree of pleasure."

"Yes," I said. "This much you have taught me. Show me more, darling. Show me more—"

She did.

With her gentle, soft, searching hands. With the edges of her nails. With her darting tongue, and questing lips, even her nibbling teeth ….

At midnight the phone jangled frantically.

It was Toussaint. "How long will it take you to get ready, Tom? Things are shaping up."

"Ten minutes," I said. I was ready a minute ahead of time and waited on the street for them.

The ride to the little flat was accomplished in silence as they were sleepy and I deep in thought. I was so tense that my back ached and before we arrived, I felt like leaping from the car and running in order to burn up my eagerness. If this strategy worked, I could see surcease from my melancholia although even with success imminent a word of warning was whispered in my ear by the caution I had bought so dearly. I strove to shove excessively rosy thoughts into mental darkness without much success but before I earned a headache from the effort, we pulled up to the curb, a block from the flat, and stopped. Keeping in the shadows, we skulked toward the building and dressed as we were, in dark clothes, we would have been hard to spot. In any case, the street seemed deserted. We climbed creaky stairs to the back door and Edwa knocked lightly.

The door opened and we walked in. Palmar was being walked around the room with Kent holding him up almost by main strength. All his chipper assurance had gone, he looked as though he had been through an ordeal. His face seemed to have shrunk, was now etched with deep lines and great purple patches that extended from his eyes down to his cheek bones.

"Sleep," he whimpered, "please, please, lemme sleep ... just one little bit of a nap ... please ... please ... please."

His head drooped forward and a snore sounded from between his loose lips. Kent gave him a shake that rattled his teeth and started walking him again. He continued whining like a badly beaten child and begging piteously for sleep.

"Put him in a chair, Kent," ordered Edwa.

The Negro let him slump into a hard-backed straight chair where he instantly fell asleep. Edwa slapped him awake and said, "Listen to what I have to say, Palmar, and you can have some sleep ... do you hear me?"

Palmar held his eyes open with difficulty. "Please ... sleep ... do anything."

Edwa in a few words outlined his idea and Palmar nodded drunkenly. "Anything, just let ..."

His head drooped forward and he was asleep again. We took him to the car and dumped him into the back seat where he fell loosely and immediately began to snore.

"How did you boys come down?" asked Pitt.

"We used your car, sir," said Hardy.

"All right. We're all through here and you can go home now if you want to and thanks a lot."

They left us and as we pulled away, I got a glimpse of their broad backs disappearing down the street. We wound around in the dimly lit streets of the Vieux Carré for a while, finally stopping before a house that was hemmed in on both sides by other houses like it. Edwa got out and went to the door, pushing a bell we could not see from the car. After some time, the door opened and a light went on, revealing an ancient crone whose ugliness was a shock.

"Hi, Mom!" said Edwa cheerily. "I had hoped it wouldn't be in the middle of the night but I had to wait till the time was ripe."

The crone cackled gleefully. "You devil, you. Come on in, all of you. We'll fix things up good, then I'll make you all some coffee."

"No one bothered my camera?"

"Indeed not," she said sharply. "I threatened to poison anyone who touched it."

"And Lottie is agreeable?"

"Lottie'll do what I say."

By that time we had hauled the whimpering Palmar up on the porch and the old woman opened the screen door for us.

"Bring him in here," she said, leading the way through the dim ancient hall into a bedroom that must have been decorated some time in the eighteen hundreds. The bed, however, was a treasure of spooled cherrywood and had been well kept.

Pitt sat Palmar on the bed and again he keeled over asleep, the old lady cackling gleefully.

She rummaged in an antique armoire and brought forth a press camera with flash attachments and several extra bulbs, handing them to Edwa. Hobbling toward the door, she said, "I'll wake Lottie."

Palmar snored blissfully on the bed while Edwa adjusted the camera and screwed in a flash bulb.

In a few minutes she came back, followed by a yawning girl of possibly eighteen, possessed of a gaudy collection of rich ripe bodily attractions. Her robe managed to cover, but could never have subdued, their outlines. She was too full blown to be called beautiful but she was pretty enough and it was certain that what she lacked in quality, she more than made up in quantity. She came in and sat on the bed. She looked Palmar over with sleepy brown eyes, her hair tumbling thickly over her shoulders.

"Geez," she muttered, "what a creep!" She smiled at Edwa, her full pouting lips curving away from white even teeth. "It's a good thing it's you, Mr. Toussaint. I wouldn't get in bed with that jerk for a thousand dollars, on my own."

Toussaint grinned and winked at me. "We all appreciate it, Lottie and if it'll embarrass you, we'll set the camera and let Mom take the picture."

The girl shrugged. "If I'm gonna be raw in front of him, why should I mind my friends being present? I'll tell you though, if he gets fresh, I'm gonna clip him one."

"He's too groggy to know what's going on," said the old woman.

Pitt busied himself stripping Palmar and when the last garment was removed, he slapped him awake.

"Please ... sleep," he mumbled.

"Hold yourself awake for ten minutes, Palmar," said Edwa, "and then you can sleep till next year if you want to."

It must be recorded that Palmar strove valiantly to do as he was told. Lottie stripped off her robe without concern for the men present and flopped into bed with him. For ten or fifteen minutes she submitted to a series of poses which made sweat break out on me.

The old woman, noticing my perturbation, laid a kindly hand on my arm. "Come on with me, son, and we'll make some coffee."

I followed her through the musty old house to a kitchen that must have been hundreds of years old. She gave me a chair and turned on the gas, placing an old cast-iron kettle of water over the flame.

"Did that brute of an Edwa ever tell you how a swell like him ever come to know an old witch like me?"

I shook my head. "No, and without meaning any disrespect, I had wondered about that."

"You don't have to mind my feelings, son, nobody else does. Well, it was nearly eight years ago... right after the war. I was walking down Conti Street and I come to a light. Seeing that it was green, I walked on across and I guess maybe, me being old and slow, I took too long and the light changed. Anyhow, somebody whizzed by and just barely grazed me, but I ain't very strong and I bet I don't weigh eighty pounds and it knocked me sprawling in the gutter. Edwa outran the guy, rammed him into a light pole, wrecking the car, then he pulled him out of it and came within an inch of beating him to death. Then he came back where I was... I was scared to death and too weak from the blow to walk and I was setting right on the curb where I was hit. Well, he came back there and if I had been his own grandmother, he couldn't have been kinder to me. He took me in his car and brought me home. Every now and then, I get a whoppin' big bill, like on Christmas and my birthday and Mardi Gras and times like that. He ain't never admitted sending them, but I know he does. He's as tender-hearted as a child and yet you get him roused up and he's hell on wheels. They tell me that that big blond man is just like him. They always comes to see me when they're in the city and I make *café brulot* for 'em and do they love it! One time they threw a big surprise party for me and you never saw the like of presents and stuff. They paid my only son's way all the way from the coast so's he could be here... he's Lottie's daddy, but she don't get along with her stepma so she lives with me. She's crazy about Edwa so she didn't mind doing this job for him. However, she really wishes it could have been him in bed instead of that fellow... and nobody around." She cackled dustily and began to drip the coffee. The others came in, Pitt grinning and Lottie and Edwa howling with laughter about something. She was hanging onto Edwa's arm and her bulging breasts were within inches of coming from under their carelessly draped covering. She whispered something in Edwa's ear and giggled.

He whispered back and she drew away archly. "You promise?"

"Cross my heart," he swore.

"All right," she said with a pout. "I'm gonna hold you to it."

When we got back to Dang's, I was so nervous I wanted to scream and Roland, who never misses anything, noticed it. He took an envelope from his pocket and handed it to me. "Take this capsule before you go to bed and you'll sleep. I brought it along for Sunny because she has been having a little trouble sleeping since the baby came, but I believe you need it more."

I tried to thank them.

"Dry up, Tom, before I bust you one," growled Edwa, drawing back a ponderous fist. I cringed away from them and in a spirit of fun, I dashed up the steps to my place and thanked them from a distance, ducking through my door when they started in my direction.

CHAPTER SIXTEEN

LOVER COME BACK

I SLEPT until ten o'clock the next morning and when I awoke I heard noises in the kitchen. I immediately assumed that they were made by Valentine, till I noticed that they were too many. Recalling that Valentine is very quiet while preparing breakfast, I frowned and put on my robe. I walked through the dinette and, for the third time in my life, came abruptly face to face with Lenthe.

I must have gaped at her for some time. At last she put down a dish and ran into my arms. I held her till my arms ached and my throat seemed ready to burst. Tears flowed from my eyes as I stroked her hair, muttering over and over: "You've come back to me, come back to me."

She raised her head trying to keep from crying, biting her lips, her chin trembling and her great soft eyes glistening with tears. Finally, she could stand it no longer and she rested her head on my chest and cried like a hurt child. She clutched the sleeves of my robe tightly, her head moving from side to side.

"I was such a fool, Tom... not to tell you in the first place. Then I was a fool again when I pretended not to know you, but I was afraid... afraid for my money. I so wanted to get rid of Palmar and he was trying so hard to get something on me in order to block my divorce action. I'm bitterly, bitterly sorry that I caused you so much suffering."

"It's all in the past and I don't want to hear any more about it."

She lifted her face and kissed me with such passion that I had to steady myself against the door. She drew away, her lips trembling from her bruising efforts. Her hands touched my face with an adorable caress, sliding down to creep beneath my robe and around my back. She hugged me hard for a moment then raised her face again. "Do you know what I want, Thomas?"

In answer, I swept her up and carried her into my room.

"We have to go to the Danglos' for lunch. I accepted and they might come looking for us."

I drew her close to me and lunch or not, interruption or not, there were things of vastly greater importance to take care of. It was twenty minutes later before we got up and dressed.

After lunch, the Toussaints and Rolands prepared to leave. Sunny came over and shook my hand with a firm grip. "Glad to see you pulled out of it, Tom. I knew you had it in you."

"Without you people, as well as many others, Sunny, I'm afraid I'd have never made it. Your Judo was as effective on me as it was on Dang."

"When's this marriage coming off?" blared Edwa, slugging me a blow on the shoulder that came within an inch of knocking me down.

As soon as I could regain my equilibrium, I answered. "It won't be more than six or seven weeks. Lenthe is going to Reno."

"You going along?"

I shook my head. "She says no. It wouldn't look good and might cause complications."

"I don't want to have to send up smoke signals for you two any more," put in Lenthe, smiling gayly.

"He'll survive for six weeks."

"We want in on it," said Pitt, grinning broadly. "It's an occasion for a party unless you are going to perform one of those

great monuments to the divorce rate, that wholly American horror known as the honeymoon usually ending in Niagara Falls."

"I agree with Mr. Roland without reserve," I said with unaccustomed vigor. "On a honeymoon there are two people cast
upon strangers in strange surroundings, and, in a sense, they
themselves are strangers. From a psychological viewpoint, it is
a deplorable way to begin a marriage. The principals are weary,
worn, trying to sleep in strange beds under new conditions and
achieve some sort of compatibility. It is remarkable that more
wrecks do not occur."

"That's my point," said Pitt. "I suppose the fashion was born
of a desire to escape hecklers, but I've always thought that a home
atmosphere with some intelligent cooperation would be a lot better for both."

"You two crusaders can compare notes at the wedding," said
Toussaint. "We gotta make tracks now." He picked up the Roland
child roughly and made a frightful face at it, the infant grinning
and pawing the big man.

So with good-natured chaffing, many promises and extrac-
tion of promises, they departed and I felt that it had been my
privilege to meet a group of the most remarkable people with
whom I was ever destined to associate.

CHAPTER SEVENTEEN
WEDDED BLISS

THE wedding took place after the allotted time had elapsed and it was no more than fitting that the clergyman who performed the ceremony be the one whose talk had been of so much value to me. The Toussaints were there, as were the Rolands, the Danglos, Aunt Cam, Joan Cannon, Dr. Crosby. In the background were Aunt Cam's excellent cook and Josy. Valentine did not attend and I never asked her why because I could think of too many good reasons myself.

The little man looked over the assembly as we stood before him and his eyes twinkled. "Some of you I know and others I do not. However, I'm going to do something I have always wanted to do. I do not believe it will affect the validity of the marriage, the legal weight being borne by the signed certificate. There may be some among you who will not appreciate my act, but I rather doubt it. In the conventional marriage, there is a lot of mumbo-jumbo ritual which does not in itself constitute a glue binding the principals together. Instead, it provides them both with ammunition which on innumerable occasions has been hurled back and forth in bitterness and recrimination. Both are asked to swear by everything they hold good and holy, that such and thus will be true fifty years hence, without providing even a suggestion as to how this is to be accomplished. In short, it is coercion. Men and women are forced to swear to things in the future without being able to know what might happen to them.

Who can see what the future will bring and what ritual can be just and productive of truth without prescience? What ritual can look into the hearts of men and women, there to see a true picture of what it is asking? I will only ask, therefore, that you be not surprised at a little changing of the questions when I come to them."

The little man then delivered a talk of philosophic richness and strange beauty. Not once did he invoke the deity and not once did he request us to humble ourselves before some heavenly majesty. Finally he reached the point of going through the ritualistic questions.

"Will you, Thomas McBride, take this woman to be your lawful wedded wife, to have and to hold ..."

He went through the whole thing and I was beginning to wonder what changes he had mentioned when finally, he was through and there was nothing to do but pronounce us man and wife." He then added:

"Do you, Thomas McBride Tallant and you, Lenthe Elizabeth Kensington, agree to bend your efforts and to the best of your ability strive to achieve the purpose of man and woman being joined in wedlock, realizing that only by mutual labor to a common end can this be achieved and understanding that no words of magic at the time of joining can quench the fires of dissension in years to come?"

In spite of our surprise, we both uttered our "I do's" with gusto.

"Then, may the intelligence which makes you see the wisdom of this reminder, and the love which brought you together, hold you so forever." He nodded at us, smiling his gentle wise smile and said, "I now pronounce you man and wife."

The men swamped Lenthe and the women performed a like office upon me. I was glad that things were thus divided because Miss Cannon kissed me with such sweet, damp abandon that I reeled.

"I ought to tell on you," she whispered in my ear, making a fiery blush mount to my cheek, which caused much humorous comment.

After the furor had died down, we repaired to Aunt Cam's house where a celebration went into full operation. Lenthe sought me and whispered. "Have you noticed there is no evidence of cruel pranks, no wasting of rice...nothing but kindness and good fellowship."

"I have indeed," I said, "and it is something we might have expected. We happen to be in the midst of civilzed people, not barbarians."

We then became separated and Aunt Cam caught me by the sleeve. She pointed to Miss Cannon who was having an uproarious session with Toussaint, their laughter ringing from the high ceiling.

"That's the girl, isn't it?" I caught her meaning instantly.

I smiled and nodded. "Yes, you are now looking at the magician who caused Phoenix Tallant to rise from his sterile ashes and become a man of substance and senses. I didn't know, Aunt Cam, that man could exist in such total separation from his nature."

"You weren't separated from it," she said curtly. "You had slugged it to sleep. Joan Cannon wakened it."

EPILOGUE

HARDLY think I should close this chronicle without telling a few things more and making a few conclusions of which the new Tallant is now acutely aware.

In a short three months, I had been converted from a man whose name was Tallant, to a man with talent, if you will excuse the pun. From a mechanical repeater of bromides and the efforts of other men, I became a man who could carry on a series of thought processes to a quick and logical end. I cannot say who helped me most as it seems they were all important, one as the other.

Aunt Cam, with her generosity and restraint, her wisdom and the desire to see me attain full stature.

Josy, with her bold flaunting of her gorgeous body, putting fire to tinder that had all but lost its inflammability.

Miss Cannon, whose cruel penetration and unflagging intent dragged me bodily from the mazes of stagnation into which I had sunk.

Danglos, with his battering-ram logic and willingness to give time and effort that a fellow man might live.

Valentine, whose selfless generosity and strange unearthly beauty gave me strength and whose affection and kindness were balm for my bruised spirit.

Toussaint and Roland, who were willing to give their time and effort to a total stranger in order that happiness could prevail.

Sunny, whose scorching and powerful personality was no less willing to drag a man from the depths and work for his heart's desire.

The strange little clergyman, who placed service above sermon and need before doctrine.

Joan Cannon is married now to a man of some means who regards her with the frank adoration one usually reserves for a deity. She has a child who has taken the brassy edge from her, mellowed and enriched her life.

Valentine married three months after I did and all of us were present. The groom is an executive in an insurance firm, a graduate of Ohio State and a handsome, broad-shouldered man whose face reflects calm dignity and purpose, whose position as a Negro has neither embittered him nor made him defensive and cynical.

As I bring this to a close, I must mention that my own happiness could hardly be improved upon. Lenthe and I live with Aunt Cam, who has gladly turned the house over to her and stands as living proof that two women can live in the same home together without friction, the matter being one of personalities rather than propinquity. I am attending the Tulane Medical School with psychiatry in view since I want to know everything possible about the human. I hope to finish my course in a shorter time than is usual because I have already covered much of the ground. While I think of it, I must correct an impression I gave at the beginning of this chronicle. I said never to have a private detective as a friend and I now wish to amend it to state that if you ever have a chance to acquire a friend like Eugene Danglos and fail to do so, you will at that moment have made the biggest mistake of your lifetime.

My pedanticism gradually loses its stiffness and disappears and I even speak like a human and not like a machine.

I am very anxious to begin practice and I intend that most of my work, if not all, shall be charity. I cannot see charging a fee for easing torture.

It is my hope that you will never need me, but if you do, I shall always be ready to serve you.

THE END